"I should have given you something to sleep in," Linc said.

"No need." It was much too easy to imagine slipping one of Linc's T-shirts over her head. Of course, it had been a fantasy that had fueled her teenage self for a long time. "It's one night. I'm fine like this."

"Have you slept at all?"

She nodded and stood. The spacious nursery felt much too close. "I think I'll fix Layla a small bottle. Maybe she'll sleep afterward. You want to hold her?"

He immediately shoved his hands into his front pockets.

She averted her eyes from the fine line of dark hair running downward from the flat indent of his navel and headed toward the doorway. "I'll take that as a no."

"She's happy with you."

He flipped on lights as they made their way to the kitchen. Before Maddie could mix up more formula, Linc did.

She sat on one of the bar stools at the island and watched.

And wondered some more.

About him and Jax.

About the nursery.

About how the bare skin stretching over his shoulders would feel beneath her fingertips...

* * *

RETURN TO THE DOUBLE C: Under the big blue Wyoming sky, this family discovers true love

Dear Reader,

Maddie Templeton bakes when she's stressed out, and when she finds herself becoming entangled with Lincoln Swift and the sweet baby that lands on his doorstep, she's definitely stressed! But her chocolate brownies soothe even the man she'd long believed to be a beast, so I thought I'd share Maddie's recipe with you!

6 oz unsweetened baking chocolate
2 oz semisweet baking chocolate
½ cup butter
3 eggs
1 cup sugar
¾ cups flour
½ tsp baking powder
¼ tsp salt
½ tsp vanilla
Powdered sugar

Melt chocolates and butter over low heat. Cool. Meanwhile, beat eggs for five minutes. Add sugar and beat again. Sift together dry ingredients and mix into egg mixture. Add melted chocolate mixture and vanilla. Spread in greased 9x13 pan and bake at 350ºC for twenty minutes. Cool slightly and dust with powdered sugar, then cut and remove from pan before entirely cool.

Happy reading, and the happiest of holiday seasons to you!

Allison

Yuletide Baby Bargain

Allison Leigh

HARLEQUIN SPECIAL EDITION®

Recycling programs
for this product may
not exist in your area.

ISBN-13: 978-0-373-62388-4

Yuletide Baby Bargain

Copyright © 2017 by Allison Lee Johnson

Printed in U.S.A.

A frequent name on bestseller lists, **Allison Leigh**'s high point as a writer is hearing from readers that they laughed, cried or lost sleep while reading her books. She credits her family with great patience for the time she's parked at her computer, and for blessing her with the kind of love she wants her readers to share with the characters living in the pages of her books. Contact her at allisonleigh.com.

Books by Allison Leigh

Harlequin Special Edition

Return to the Double C

Vegas Wedding, Weaver Bride
A Child Under His Tree
The BFF Bride
One Night in Weaver...
A Weaver Christmas Gift
A Weaver Beginning
A Weaver Vow
A Weaver Proposal
Courtney's Baby Plan
The Rancher's Dance

The Fortunes of Texas: The Secret Fortunes

Wild West Fortune

The Fortunes of Texas: All Fortune's Children

Fortune's Secret Heir

The Fortunes of Texas: Cowboy Country

Fortune's June Bride

Montana Mavericks: 20 Years in the Saddle!

Destined for the Maverick

Men of the Double C Ranch

A Weaver Holiday Homecoming
A Weaver Baby
A Weaver Wedding

Visit the Author Profile page at Harlequin.com for more titles.

For beautiful little Monroe Lea,
who has been born into a wonderful family.
Welcome to the world!

Chapter One

"Are you a social worker or not?"

Maddie Templeton's jaw tightened at the impatient words being spat at her through the phone line. She wished she could pretend she didn't recognize the owner of the voice.

This was the last thing she needed. She'd already spent the entire day dealing with tying up troublesome details at work before a forced two-week vacation. Then she'd rushed home to change into somewhat date-worthy clothing and driven the thirty miles over winding roads from Braden to Weaver, where she was supposed to meet a man named Morton for dinner.

Only Morton had stood her up.

Instead of having a date for the first time in months—which was a generous estimate, if she were truthful—she'd ended up spending the evening with her grandmother. Not that Vivian wasn't entertaining enough. She just wasn't the kind of company that Maddie had been hoping for.

Now, it was after ten o'clock, and after returning to the house she shared with her sisters—knowing *they* were probably out with guys who'd never dream of standing them up—she just didn't feel in the mood to deal with Lincoln Swift's phone call.

Because she couldn't stand Lincoln Swift.

If only she'd let the phone continue ringing as she'd walked in the door. Eventually, it would have gone to voice mail, and she'd be happily trespassing in Greer's bathroom by now, watching her sister's claw-foot tub fill with hot water while she decided what task to tackle first on her use-it-or-lose-it vacation time.

Instead, she leaned against the half-finished kitchen cabinets—the do-it-yourself refinishing job had been stalled for months—and fantasized about hanging up on him. After telling him just how little she thought of him.

After all these years, turnabout *would* be sweet.

But instead of letting every bit of her day's frustration out on the man, she swallowed it down. "Yes, Linc, I am a social worker," she said evenly. "What's the problem?" There would *have* to be a problem to make Linc ever reach out to the likes of her.

"I don't want to get into it on the phone. Just come to the house."

"I'm sorry." Even though her teeth clenched and her hand tightened around the receiver, she managed to channel the dulcet tone that Greer used in the courtroom before skewering someone. "What house?"

As if Maddie didn't know perfectly well that he'd moved into the grand old mansion once owned by his grandmother, Ernestine Swift, after her death. Maddie knew every corner of that mansion, too. But only because as a child, she'd accompanied her mother every week when Meredith cleaned the place for Ernestine.

That was how she'd met Linc and his brother, Jax, in the first place.

They'd chased each other all over that place.

Until Linc had decided he was too old for such nonsense and pretty much seemed to forget Maddie existed.

Then it had been just Jax and Maddie.

Until Linc had decided *that* was nonsense, too.

"My brother's gone and done it again." Linc's voice was tight. "Are you going to help me or not?"

When she and Jax had dated, they'd been in high school, but even then Maddie hadn't been serious about him. He was a lot of fun. But good boyfriend material? Definitely not.

Aside from her sisters, though, he'd been just about her best friend in the world. Until Linc made sure she knew she wasn't good enough for Jax in any way, shape or form.

That had been thirteen years ago, and it still held the record as the single most humiliating moment of her life—far outstripping being stood up by a computer programmer named Morton.

She dropped the dulcet tones for her usual frankness. "Jax is thirty years old, Linc. He's a grown man. Whatever he's gone and done, he can undo." Jax had had plenty of practice, after all. And it wouldn't be legal trouble. If it were, Linc definitely wouldn't have called her. Swift Oil, his family business, had a phalanx of lawyers on the payroll.

"He's not *here.* He's out of town." Linc sounded like he was talking through his teeth, too, and it took no effort at all to conjure an image of his face.

Which annoyed her to no end.

Even though she ran into Jax fairly often around town, she'd had only a few dealings with Linc since that long-ago mortifying day.

He ran an oil company.

She was a social worker.

Since he'd moved back to Braden when his grandmother died, they'd rarely run into each other. Which was saying something because, on a good day, the population there didn't break 5,000. The last time she'd seen him in person had been at Ernestine's funeral. Three years ago.

She'd offered her condolences and left the very second that she could.

She squared up the stack of paint chips sitting on the counter that her sisters had been squabbling over for a month, trying to block the memory of the grief that she'd seen in his face that day. "If Jax isn't there, then what are you even calling me for?"

"Because his kid *is* here," he said even more sharply. "Isn't that what you deal with? Kids left to fend for themselves because their parents can't be bothered?"

She straightened abruptly from her slouch, and felt her red sweater catch on a nail. He could have been describing his and Jax's parents, but she had the sense not to point that out. She carefully unhooked the threads of her sweater before they unraveled. "Jax has a child?" She knew she sounded shocked, even though it wasn't such a shocking thought.

Jax loved women, after all. He'd never been without at least one on his arm from the time he'd entered puberty. But he'd always claimed he'd never get caught by one the way his dad had been.

Linc made a sound that wasn't quite an oath. "Just

get over here, would you please? I didn't know who else to call."

She grimaced. "You must be desperate, indeed."

"I'll leave the gate open," he said flatly.

A moment later, all she heard was the dial tone.

He'd hung up on her.

"I'll leave the gate open," she muttered, hanging up harder than necessary. Typical Linc. Issuing edicts as if he had a divine right to do so.

It would serve him right if she ignored him. She *was* supposed to be on vacation, after all.

But what about the child?

Jax's child?

She huffed out a breath and left the kitchen, returning to the foyer where she'd left her boots. The artificial Christmas tree that her sister Ali bought was sitting in its enormous box, blocking half the room. None of them were thrilled with having an artificial tree instead of a fresh-cut one, but Ali's overdeveloped sense of safety had prevailed. She was a police officer and had just dealt with a family home burning down from a tree that went up in flames. Neither Greer nor Maddie had had the heart to argue with her. They'd both promised Ali they'd help put it up this weekend.

Maddie sat down on the box, pulled on her leather boots and zipped them up to her knees.

Despite the weatherman's dire predictions, it still hadn't snowed yet, but the temperatures were already cold and bitter. She wrapped a scarf around her neck on top of her coat before she let herself back out into the night. Her car was parked in the driveway; both engine and interior were still warm from the drive back from Weaver.

At least she wouldn't have to go so far to get to the

old Swift mansion. It used to sit on the eastern edge of Braden, but due to progress, the town limits had been creeping past it for years. Now it was more like a crown jewel in the center of town.

When she arrived, the ornate iron gate guarding the long drive to the house was open, just as Linc had promised.

She drove through it, and memories of climbing on the thing pulled at her. The first time, Maddie's mother had been horrified. But Ernestine—seeming old even then—had merely laughed and waved it off. How could Maddie be expected to not climb on it when her grandsons were doing the same thing?

Maddie rubbed her forehead, trying and failing to block out the images of her, Jax and Linc running around that first summer. She and Jax had been six, Linc a much older and wiser eleven.

By the time she and Jax were eleven, Meredith was no longer cleaning the mansion for Ernestine. But Maddie's friendship with Jax—and her fascination with Linc, who'd totally lost interest in them by that point—had lived on. For a few more years, anyway. Until he'd made so very plain what he thought of her.

Her headlights swept over the stone wall that ran alongside the narrow driveway as it curved its way to the mansion sitting atop the hill.

Her mouth felt dry.

Which was just plain stupid.

The drive swelled out into a circle in front of the house before narrowing again as it continued off into the darkness. She hadn't been out there in more than a decade, but she assumed there was still an enormous detached garage next to the gardener's shack.

She parked in the circle and took a deep breath before

getting out of the car and reluctantly climbing the brick steps. As soon as she reached the door, she could hear the wailing from inside and her gloved hand paused on the lion-shaped doorknocker.

It was the distinct wail of a baby.

She started when the door opened, the doorknocker yanked out of her lax fingers before she could even properly use it.

"Took you long enough," Linc greeted her as he shoved the infant car seat he was holding into her arms.

She rapidly adjusted her hold on it when he let go and backed away. Like he couldn't get away fast enough.

From the baby? Or from Maddie?

She averted her gaze, but not fast enough to keep from noticing that his disheveled blondish-brown hair showed a sprinkle of gray on the sides that hadn't been there three years ago, and the faint lines arrowing out from the corners of his hazel eyes weren't quite so faint anymore.

And he looked better than ever.

Dammit.

She channeled Greer's dulcet tones again. "Good to see you, too, Linc." She smiled insincerely and looked down at the wailing baby. A girl, if the pink blanket was anything to go by. "Where's her mom?"

"Who the hell knows?" He shoved his long fingers through his hair. "I came home and that—" he waved at the infant seat "—was sitting all alone on the doorstep."

She stepped inside and set the carrier on the old-fashioned table in the middle of the spacious foyer. After dumping her purse on the table, too, she delved beneath the pink blanket, relieved to feel warmth coming off the crying baby. "How long ago?"

"You're not shocked?"

She deftly released the harness strapping the baby into the seat and picked her up. "By a baby being left somewhere or by *you* calling *me* about it?" She didn't wait for his answer as she tried to soothe the baby. "Unfortunately, I can't say this is my first experience with an abandoned baby. How long ago did you get home?"

He was wearing a dark blazer over a white shirt and blue jeans. Date wear.

She hated the fact that she'd even noticed. Or that she cared.

The baby was still wailing, so hard that she was hiccupping. "It's okay, sweetheart." Maddie jiggled the baby and blindly swept her hand inside the car seat, finally finding a pacifier wedged under a corner of the fabric lining. She touched it to the baby's lips and she latched on to it greedily.

"Silence," Linc muttered. "Thank God."

Maddie refrained from telling him that he could have found the pacifier, too, if he'd tried. Through the fleecy polka-dotted sleeper the baby was wearing, she could feel the diaper was heavy. "So? How long ago?"

"Less than an hour ago." Linc raked his fingers through his hair again and paced on the other side of the foyer table. "A few minutes before I called you the first time. It took three tries before you bothered to answer."

"Don't make it sound like *I've* done something wrong," she said. "I was out, too. It is allowed, you know. Even for social workers."

And those too lowly to consort with the vaunted Swift family.

She pressed her lips against the child's temple, banishing the thought.

The baby's forehead felt sweaty, but that could have

just been from all her crying. "Is there a diaper bag or something?"

"Or something." He set a small plastic garbage bag on the table next to the car seat.

Maddie quickly reached for it and their hands accidentally brushed. She ignored the heat that immediately ran under her skin and tipped the bag over. A half-dozen diapers and a thin container of baby wipes scattered across the table. A small can of powdered baby formula and an empty, capped baby bottle rolled out.

She grabbed a diaper and the wipes and marched around the table, heading into the house. "Go make a bottle with the formula," she told him. "I'll get her diaper changed, and then I'll call my uncle."

Linc stared after Maddie's departing form. Her hair was as dark as it had always been, but it was longer now than she'd used to wear it, tumbling well past the bright red scarf wrapped around the collar of her short black coat. Below the coat, her hips—trim as ever— were outlined in black denim jeans tucked into her flat-heeled brown boots.

She always had liked wearing boots. Not the cowboy kind, either.

He grabbed the container of formula and the bottle. Not that he knew what to do with them. "Why do you want to call your uncle?"

"He's a pediatrician," she answered as if it should be obvious. She'd laid the baby on the antique bench situated against one wall of the living room. Even though the baby's legs and arms were waving around, Maddie competently peeled back the neck-to-toe outfit, revealing a tiny white T-shirt that didn't reach past the baby's rosy belly and a fat-looking disposable diaper. "Poor thing is soaked." She sent him a chastising look as she slipped a fresh diaper under the existing one.

"Save that look for the person who dumped off the kid on my front porch."

She pulled out a wet wipe from the plastic container. "How long do you think she'd been there before you got home?"

"God only knows." His first reaction when he'd realized what was on his porch had been to call the police. He'd had his phone in his hands when he'd spotted the note tucked next to the kid's head.

After reading it, he'd learned that the little girl's name was Layla and that she belonged to Jax. Supposedly. Which meant there was no way he could call the police.

And there was no way to reach Jax, either, since he'd found his brother's cell phone sitting dead in the kitchen where Jax had forgotten it.

He'd found the phone a week ago.

But his brother had been gone longer than that.

He focused on the top of Maddie's head while she undid the wet diaper.

He knew she still hated him. And why. But even if he'd had to do things over again, he would still choose the same path.

"I was busy all day at the office. Worked there until about seven, then went straight on to a dinner engagement." It was as good a way as any to describe the irritating evening spent with his parents. They'd thrown a party, celebrating their thirty-fifth wedding anniversary.

Linc might have celebrated it, too, if he didn't know what a joke their marriage really was. If Blake Swift wasn't cheating on Jolene, then Jolene was cheating on

Blake. Except for the delight they took in making each other miserable, Linc still couldn't understand why they remained together. He also would have accused Jax of making a getaway before the party, except Linc knew perfectly well that his brother couldn't care less what their parents did.

"There was nobody here at the house to notice anything?"

"No."

She'd finished diapering the baby. She kept her palm on the baby's chest as she glanced up at him. "No?"

He frowned. Her pretty eyes were as dark as chocolate and yet the doubt in them was as clear as a spotlight. Another thing that hadn't changed over the years. Everything going on inside Maddie's head was broadcast through those expressive eyes. Her two sisters had the exact same eyes—the exact same looks, in fact, since they were identical triplets—but he'd never thought their emotions were as transparent as Maddie's.

And he'd never looked at Greer or Ali and felt a slow burn inside.

"Who do you think *should* have been here?"

She looked back at the baby. "I figured you'd have a housekeeper or something." She slipped the baby's kicking legs back into her stretchy clothes. "At least she seems to have been warm enough. I don't see any signs of frostbite. She still needs an exam, though." She folded the used diaper and wipe into a ball, secured it with the sticky diaper tapes and held it out.

He was glad his hands were full. He lifted them—formula can in one, empty bottle in the other.

She rolled her eyes and picked up the baby, nestling her in one arm as she stood. "Kitchen still in the same place?" Not waiting for an answer, she walked past him and around the staircase.

He followed. "Where would it have gone?"

She ignored the question. When she reached the kitchen, she tossed the diaper into the trash bin located in the walk-in pantry, then returned to stop in front of him. She took the can from his fingers and set it on the wide soapstone-topped island. Then she took the bottle and before he knew it, she was holding out the baby.

Layla watched him with wide blue eyes. She was going at the pacifier as if it might actually produce milk.

"Oh for heaven's sake, Linc!" Maddie sounded exasperated. "Just take her. She won't break."

He wasn't so sure. He gingerly placed his hands near Maddie's, underneath the baby's arms. As soon as he did, Maddie moved hers away. She went to the sink and turned on the water to wash her hands.

The baby was a lot lighter than he expected, considering how heavy she'd been when strapped inside the car seat.

She opened her mouth, the pacifier dropped out and she let out an ear-piercing wail. For such a tiny thing, she made a helluva racket.

He wasn't a man who panicked easily, yet that was all he'd done since he'd realized there was a baby on his doorstep.

"Nope." He pushed the kid back at Maddie. "No way."

"Oh, for the love of Pete." She took the baby back. "Get me the pacifier."

It had rolled under the scrolled wooden edge of the island. He grabbed it, handing it to her.

"Wash it, would you please?" She handed him the bottle. "And this, too."

He joined her at the sink. "Aren't they supposed to be sterilized or something?"

"In a perfect world, probably. But who knows what other conditions this baby has endured. For now, hot water and a good wash with soap will have to do." Without waiting for him to finish washing the pacifier and bottle, she tucked one wet finger into the baby's mouth.

The crying stopped.

But that was the only bit of relief he got.

"Now that my hands are busy, you can make her a bottle," Maddie ordered. "Directions are on the side of the can."

He peered at the small print on the can. He'd left his reading glasses in his jacket and it was impossible to read.

Maddie was pacing around the island, bouncing the baby a little with each step. "How do you know for sure she's Jax's baby, anyway? Do you know her name?"

"Layla. And of course she's Jax's."

"He told you?"

"He didn't have to." Glad for the excuse, he left the can on the counter and went back out to the foyer. When he returned, he had his reading glasses as well as the note. He unfolded it and spread it on the counter so she could see. "This was stuck in the car seat with her."

Maddie pursed her lips as she studied the single line of looping handwriting. "Jaxie, please take care of Layla for me," she read. Her eyes lifted to his for a moment. "Jaxie?"

"You know how women are with Jax." Even Maddie had been susceptible to his brother, once. Until Linc set her straight.

"The note isn't signed."

He gave her a look. "Presumably, *Jaxie* knows who the mother of his own child is."

"But he obviously didn't tell you about her."

"Yeah, well, we don't really talk to each other a lot anymore."

"How long has he been out of town?"

He shrugged. "Little over a week."

"He still lives here, doesn't he?"

"Yes. So?"

"So how can you live in the same house and not talk to each other?"

He wished he hadn't said anything. "It's not germane."

Her eyebrows rose. "Oh. Well, if it's not *germane.*" She gave him a wide-eyed stare and grabbed the washed pacifier, trading it for the tip of her index finger in the baby's mouth. Then she took the baby bottle and filled it part way with tap water, added a few scoops from the can of formula without so much as a glance at the tiny print, and screwed on the nipple. She shook the bottle vigorously and held it under running hot water. "While you're feeding her, I'll call my uncle and check in with my boss to let him know what's going on. I have enough autonomy to set up the emergency placement, but Ray's still going to want to know about it. He's a stickler that way. But no matter where the placement ends up being, Layla still needs an exam first, particularly considering the way she was left. Just because I didn't see any signs of injury, it's not a medical assessment. And Uncle David's qualified to make one, which means maybe we can avoid having to involve the hospital, too. Are you *sure* you don't know who her mother might be?"

"If I did, I wouldn't have needed to call you." He tossed his reading glasses onto the island alongside the note. "And what the hell is 'emergency placement' supposed to mean?"

Chapter Two

Ignoring Linc's annoyed tone, Maddie turned off the water and dried the bottle with a towel she pulled from the drawer next to the sink, all with one hand. The white cloth was clean and crisp, just like the towels that Ernestine had kept there when Maddie was a child. She wondered if Linc had changed anything at all around the house since his grandmother died.

The black-framed glasses were definitely a new addition for him, though—and an unwelcome, unexpectedly sexy one.

"Emergency placement," she repeated smoothly. "It's what it sounds like." Layla's eyes were fastened on the bottle and she wrapped her little starfish hands around it as soon as Maddie put the nipple near her lips.

The baby's eyes nearly rolled back in her head as she guzzled the lukewarm formula. "Poor baby. You're so hungry." Anger threatened to boil inside her over the baby's neglect, but she knew better than to let it get the best of her. She couldn't be effective in her job if she let herself be consumed by anger or horror over the situations she saw.

When she looked at Linc again, his brows were pulled even closer together above his long, narrow nose.

She definitely shouldn't take any pleasure in antagonizing him. Not under these circumstances.

"Emergency placement is a temporary measure while the authorities have a chance to investigate the whole situation," she explained calmly. "Once that's done, our office will make the report to the prosecutor's office. If there are criminal charges involved, he'll probably handle the case. If there aren't, he'll likely leave it in our department's hands to make a recommendation to the judge—"

"Judge! Who said anything about a judge?"

She watched him for a moment. Linc had always been much harder to read than Jax. But the fact that he was more alarmed than ever was obvious. She just wasn't entirely certain why. Despite the past, he'd called her to take care of the situation, and that was what she was doing. "No matter what led to Layla being left on your doorstep, this situation is going to involve the family court," she said a little more gently. "Judge Stokes is a good guy—"

"I don't care how good a guy he is. There's no need for a judge. No need for your boss, for that matter."

"If you didn't ask me here to do my *job*, then what is it that you expect me to do?"

He gestured, encompassing her and the baby in his short, impatient wave. "What you're doing. Taking care of the kid."

"I'm not a babysitter, Linc! And this *kid* is an infant.

Two, three months old, tops, if I had to guess." She flicked the fingers of her free hand against the note still lying on the island. "And assuming that can be trusted, she also has a name. Layla. Aside from that, we know nothing for certain."

"Jax—"

"Jax isn't here. So I'll tell you the same thing Judge Stokes is going to tell you. This child appears to have been abandoned and—"

"No." He crossed the room in two strides and took the baby out of her arms.

The bottle fell out of Maddie's grasp and rolled across the table. Layla's eyes rounded and she opened her mouth to protest loudly, but he caught it before it rolled onto the floor and shoved the nipple quickly back into her mouth. The baby subsided, blissfully guzzling once again, even though Linc was essentially holding her like a football under his arm. "You're not sticking her with a bunch of strangers."

"I don't even know how to respond to that." Layla was kicking her legs so enthusiastically, Maddie was afraid the infant would squirt out from Linc's grasp like a wet bar of soap. "She's going to spit up everything she drinks. Give her to me."

"No."

She lifted her eyebrows. She wasn't a seventeen-year-old girl who could be easily brushed off by him anymore. She'd cut her teeth in adult probation before transferring into family services. *"No?"*

"If you're not going to help, then just go home." He turned away from her, walking out of the room. Layla's legs bounced.

Maddie followed after him, skipping twice to dart around him and block his momentum. "You don't get it!"

He frowned down at her. "I get that you're in my way."

"You can't unring the bell here. I can't pretend you didn't call me." She tried to slide Layla out of his grip.

He caught one of her hands in his, holding it away.

"Linc! I have a legal obligation to rep—" She broke off when he squeezed her fingers. Not enough to hurt, but enough to express himself. His hazel eyes were hard and his jaw was so tight, it looked white.

"To do nothing," he ground out. "She's my *niece*."

Maddie exhaled, feeling a sudden wave of sympathy that she hoped was more from exhaustion and good-will toward his brother than because of tender feelings for Linc himself. "You *think* she's your niece," she corrected in an even tone. Based on a note that said nothing of substance.

"She was left in my care."

"Jax's care, actually. And you're saying he's out of town. Have you tried calling him? To see what he has to say about the baby?"

"He'll be home soon." Linc's tone was flat.

She didn't believe him.

"Do you even know where he is?"

His expression turned darker, his jawline whiter. "No."

She sighed.

There was no earthly reason why she should want to help him. Yet that was exactly what she realized she was going to do. Or try to do. It would involve an end-run around her boss, but he was already going to be annoyed with her anyway, so she supposed she might as well be hung for a sheep as a lamb.

"I'll call Archer." Her brother, though personally exasperating, was a well-respected attorney practicing in Braden. "He used to clerk for Judge Stokes back in the day and they have a good relationship. Hopefully good enough to cut out some of the steps and get you appointed temporary custodian right from the start."

"Perfect."

"He can *try*. It's still a longshot," she warned. "You're a single man with no proof right now that this baby is your niece, so you don't have that relationship on your side. I'm on a first-name basis with all of the individuals around this region who are qualified foster care providers, and there's not a single, unmarried man among them. So—"

"I don't care who or what they are. I'm not some perfect stranger! Everyone in this town knows the Swift family."

Not necessarily a good thing. She kept the thought to herself. "Swift Oil pumps a lot of money into Wyoming," she allowed. "But—"

"But nothing. That should at least buy me enough time with the judge so that I can prove she's my niece!"

He wouldn't be able to buy anything else with the judge. She had plenty of experience with Horvald Stokes. The judge cared about one thing—the well-being of a child. Period. "Without the mother here to say anything, you'll need a DNA test to prove it."

"Then I'll get a freaking DNA test!" His voice rose. "How long can that take?" Layla's face crumpled and she started crying again.

And Linc looked like he was about to lose it.

Maddie decided not to tell him that Layla would need the test, as well. And that would require the judge's order, too. "I'll call Archer," she said again and this time, successfully lifted the baby out of Linc's arms. She offered Layla the bottle, but the baby turned her fussy face away. Maddie put her against her shoulder as she walked back out to the foyer, rubbing her back. "It's okay, sweetie. What a night you've had, huh?"

"That's one way of putting it."

She worked open her purse and started rummaging inside. "I wasn't talking to you."

As if she would ever call *him* sweetie.

Her fingers latched on to her cell phone and she dragged it out of her purse. "When did you start needing glasses?"

She didn't bother dialing her brother's home phone. There was no way he'd be home on a Friday night. Archer was the only person she knew who liked his women more than Jaxon Swift did. Instead, she dialed his cell phone and hoped that he would at least be somewhere that the signal reached. Around their area of the state, such a thing was never guaranteed.

"Why?"

She tucked the phone against her shoulder as she bounced the baby and started unwinding her winter scarf. "Just trying to make conversation."

"I don't need conversation. I need results." He left the foyer.

She made a face at his departing back and finally freed the scarf. She dropped it on top of her purse and started unbuttoning her coat.

"This better be good," Archer's voice suddenly came on the line. "I was in the middle of something."

"Middle of some*one* more like," she said. "I need a favor." She quickly told him the situation. "Do you mind calling the judge for me? See if he's willing to even consider it?"

"What's your boss say about it?"

She mentally crossed her fingers. "He said it's my call." As lies went, it wasn't the worst she could tell.

Under ordinary circumstances, Raymond Marx trusted Maddie's judgment.

But she had only had a few days off in the last three years. And he'd been adamant. The rules required a minimum of two continuous weeks off every year. She was well past that. Which meant that in this instance, her boss would say she was on vacation and should hand off anything even remotely approaching a case to one of her associates for the next two weeks. Period. She was supposed to be out living her life. Having a date or two. He'd even set her up with his buddy, Morton. Because, despite being a stickler for the rules, Ray really did care about his people.

"Are you going to help me or not?"

"Stay by the phone," her brother said in answer, and disconnected.

"Nothing like being surrounded by abrupt men," she murmured. She managed to shrug out of her coat and the baby finally gave up a hard little burp.

"Attagirl." Maddie shifted her hold on Layla and offered the bottle once more. "Pretty much my thinking, too, where they're concerned."

"Where who are concerned?"

Of course Linc would choose that moment to return.

She rounded the foyer table, for some reason wanting to keep it between them. "Nothing important. This looks like the same table that your grandmother had when my mother and I were here. My mom used to let me dust the base because I was always begging to help." Until she'd learned cleaning was really a chore and not a game.

"It is the same table. No reason to change it."

She chewed the inside of her cheek when silence fell and she had no brilliant ideas of how to fill it.

Fortunately, her cell phone rang just as she could feel a blush starting to rise in her cheeks. "It's Archer already." She didn't expect such a quick response to bode well, and considering the way Linc's lips thinned, she suspected he had the same feeling.

She managed to hold both Layla and the bottle with one hand as she pressed a key and held the phone to her ear. "Any luck?"

"Depends on who's asking," Archer said. She could hear music in the background. "Not surprisingly, Stokes isn't inclined to depart from usual procedure, kiddo. File a report with the sheriff and turn the baby over to the hospital until an emergency placement can be made."

She sighed, shaking her head slightly when Linc's eyes captured hers. "Well, thanks for trying. I'll get the ball rolling with the sheriff—"

"No." Linc's voice was adamant in her one ear, and Archer's "Hold on, kiddo," was cautionary in the other.

She ignored Linc for her brother. "What?"

"Being the weekend and all, Stokes suggested that *you* could personally take the child into protective custody until the hearing can be scheduled about Swift's petition. If you agree, that is."

Linc was standing still, watching her intently. She wished that he'd at least pace. Then he'd be doing something else with all that pent-up frustration besides shooting it all at her from his eyes. And maybe she'd be able to breathe more normally.

It was galling that even after all these years, just being near him made her…edgy.

Layla had drained the bottle, so Maddie set it on the table, repositioning the baby once more against her shoulder as she considered Archer's words. The hearing had to be scheduled within forty-eight hours, excluding the weekend. "At the latest, we're looking at midweek, then." At which time the judge would likely order the baby be placed into shelter care while the prosecutor's office investigated. They'd start by determining whether Layla was already reported as a missing child, and then try to locate her mother.

But to locate her, they'd need to identify her.

In the meantime, Linc would get a head start on reaching Jax. And maybe he could succeed before Ray even found out about Maddie's involvement.

"Stokes said to call his clerk Monday morning first thing," Archer told her. "The judge'll make room earlier in the schedule if it's humanly possible. It's that or emergency foster care for the next several days," he concluded.

"I'm aware of that." It wasn't as if Braden had an overabundance of qualified providers willing to take an infant on a moment's notice. The last baby she'd had to place in emergency care ended up more than fifty miles away. If a caregiver couldn't be found, the baby would be assigned to the hospital, which wasn't ideal, either. For now, Maddie did have time on her hands. And she was perfectly qualified to take care of Layla for a few days, so long as she didn't have Linc breathing down her neck the whole while.

"So? What'll it be, Maddie? He's waiting for me to call him back to confirm."

Layla burped again and then turned her head against Maddie's throat, letting out a shuddering sigh.

Maddie sighed, too. She'd always been able to keep an emotional distance when it came to children—at least professionally.

But none of the children who'd ever passed through her casework had been a relative of a friend.

Linc finally moved, but only to plant his hands flat on the foyer table while he bowed his head.

Or a former friend.

She looked away. When Ray did discover what she was doing, he would just have to understand. She might be on vacation because of him, but what she did on that vacation was entirely up to her. "Tell Judge Stokes that I agree."

"You don't sound too happy about it, kiddo."

She didn't look back at Linc. "It'll be fine." The trick would be to maintain her usual professionalism. Forget the past. Forget everything but the baby. "I appreciate the help. Sorry to interrupt your evening."

"No harm. I'll catch you Monday."

"Thanks, Archer." She ended the call.

"What hearing? What did you agree to?"

There was a mirror on one wall and she could see in it that Layla's eyes were at half-mast. She also could see that Linc had lifted his head and his eyes were dark and intense.

Professionalism. She took a quick breath and turned to him. "The judge is willing to let me take Layla into protective custody. There will be a hearing scheduled by the middle of the week, at the latest, when he'll probably order her into foster care."

"But he could leave her in my care."

"She's not in your care, Linc. She's in mine. Temporarily. What happens after that depends greatly on Judge Stokes. If he decides that placing Layla with you is in her best interests, then that's what he'll do."

"But if my DNA proves she's my niece—"

She lifted her hand. "That's going to take at least a week. Maybe more. Until then, I'm telling you not to put all your eggs in that particular basket. Because it's beyond unlikely that you'll be granted temporary custody as a foster-care provider. You're not qualified, and I know Judge Stokes. He's never done that before. He's not likely to do it now just because you *want* him to."

His lips twisted. "You're enjoying this."

She had enough experience under her belt dealing with families in turmoil to keep from losing her patience.

"There is nothing enjoyable about an abandoned child, I promise you. And maybe none of it will be necessary. Maybe you'll reach Jax. He'll come back and offer proof that he knew nothing about this situation at all. He'll claim her and everyone will be happy." Maddie turned the car seat around on the table and carefully lowered Layla into it.

Linc looked alarmed. "Where are you taking her?"

"Nowhere." Yet. "She's falling asleep and the seat is as good a place as any." She shook out the pink blanket and gently spread it over the baby before picking up her phone again.

"Now who are you calling?"

"My uncle." Because that was one thing she would not neglect.

"It's too late."

She shook her head, already finished dialing. "He's had late calls like this before. Uncle David! Hi." He'd answered on the first ring. "It's Maddie. Sorry for the late call but I have an abandoned baby—"

"She's not abandoned," Linc interjected.

She turned her back on him. "I don't know how long she was left alone outside, but I didn't see any signs of frostbite or other injury. I'm guessing somewhere between eight and twelve weeks old. But she's in my care at least through the weekend, and you know how we'll ultimately need a medical eval for her case—"

Unable to stand listening to Maddie's one-sided conversation, Linc picked up the baby—car seat and all—and carried her from the foyer.

He wasn't thrilled with the decisions being made around him. But he also knew that he didn't have much of a choice.

He bypassed the kitchen and carried the baby into his study, where he carefully set the car seat on the floor.

He sank wearily onto the couch, staring down at the baby's face. Her eyelids were closed, looking delicate and pink. Her lashes were soft feather fans of pale brown, much darker than the wisps of hair on her round little head.

He'd never been around babies. Never wanted to be, particularly after his wife got pregnant with someone else's. Dana had then become his *ex*-wife. That had been nearly six years ago.

Layla hitched in an audible breath, which made him hold his. She sucked at her bow-shaped lips and her pink eyelids fluttered.

But she didn't wake.

He exhaled slowly, and slid off the couch to sit on the floor next to the car seat.

"Linc?"

"In here." He didn't raise his voice. Maddie still must have heard, because a moment later she came into his study. She stopped when she saw him sitting on the floor.

The leather creaked as she slowly perched on the far cushion of the couch. "Are you all right?"

"They must pay you to ask." He was certain she hadn't asked out of friendly concern.

She didn't answer immediately, but slid down to sit next to him on the floor, her back against the couch. The car seat was between them. "Considering I'm on vacation, technically, I'm not really getting paid for this at all." She sounded carefully neutral.

He gave her a sideways look. "Vacation?"

"Another thing even social workers are allowed." She stretched out her legs and fiddled with the plain watch strapped around her narrow wrist. "My boss scheduled it. Told me he didn't want to see me in the office for the next two weeks."

"Big fan of yours?"

She shrugged, neither confirming nor denying.

"If you're on vacation, what are you doing here?"

"You didn't exactly give me a chance to tell you." She folded back the edge of the pink blanket with her slender fingers. Her fingernails were short, neat and unvarnished. "I work in family services, Linc. Vacation or not, this is what I do."

"You could have sent someone else."

"You called *me*. At my home. If I'd known any one of my associates would have done just as well, I'd have been more than happy to send someone else." Her fingertips grazed the downy blond hair on Layla's head. "You're stuck with me now. At least until the hearing next week." She drew her hands back and went onto her knees, wrapping her fingers around the carrier handle.

"What are you doing?"

"Right now, Layla is in my care. Which means where I go, she goes." She stood, picking up the carrier. "And I'm going home. It's been a very long day, and my uncle is going to meet me there."

"Why not here?"

"Because we're not staying here," she said with exaggerated patience.

He stood, closing his hand over hers on the handle.

She froze, her expression tightening. "Linc, don't even ask me to leave her with you."

"I wasn't going to."

Her gaze flicked up to his, then away.

"You could both stay here." He realized his hand was still on hers and let go. "You know how big this place is. There's lots of room."

"There's room at my house, too."

She lived in a worn-down Victorian that she shared with her sisters. He'd driven by it more than once. His brother's bar was nearby.

"Does it have a nursery?"

She waved her hand, taking in their surroundings. "The only thing that seems to have changed since the last time I was here is this room, and your grandmother didn't have a nursery, either."

"I've changed a few things. And she put in the nursery a few years before she died."

Maddie gave him a surprised look, but still shook her head. "A nursery isn't a necessity."

"Maybe not. And there's nothing in it but furniture, but it's better than that." He gestured at the car seat. "Better than that house of yours."

"What do you know about my house?"

"It was on the condemned list when you bought it."

"It *was* not!"

"Okay. Maybe not." He waited a beat. "If Jax asked, you'd agree."

Her lips compressed. "If Jax were here, presumably

he would know who the woman was who left Layla for him and the situation would be entirely different."

Linc's stomach burned, worse than it had when he'd called her for help in the first place. "Please."

She rested the car seat on the arm of the couch and her lashes swept down. She exhaled heavily. "Fine. But just because it's already so late." But then she sent him a skewering look. "And *just* for tonight."

If he could talk her into one night, he figured his chances were pretty good of talking her into another.

But all he did was nod. "I'll show you where the nursery is."

Chapter Three

Maddie jerked awake, staring into the dark for a second before she remembered where she was.

Under Lincoln Swift's roof.

And Layla was crying.

She pushed the button on her sensible watch and groaned a little when it lit up with the time. It hadn't even been two hours since her uncle had left.

Every muscle she possessed wanted her to roll over and curl up against the pillows.

But she shoved aside the blanket that she'd pulled over herself and climbed off the bed. Aside from removing her boots before lying down, she was still fully dressed.

The bedroom she was using connected directly to the nursery. Linc's warning about furniture being the only thing the room possessed had been accurate.

The mattress inside the spectacularly beautiful wooden

crib had no bedding. The drawers of the matching chest contained nothing but drawer liners. The changing table held no diapers.

She couldn't help but wonder if it ever had.

Only the toy box held anything of note—a stuffed bear easily as big as Layla. It was dressed in overalls and cowboy boots. Even all these years after Maddie had dusted the ornate base of the foyer table, she could remember Ernestine talking about her husband, Gus. He'd died when he was still a relatively young man. No matter what sort of success the wildcatter had found before his death, though, he'd always worn overalls and cowboy boots.

One thing Maddie was used to doing, though, was improvising. She'd folded a regular bedsheet tightly around the crib mattress and Linc had produced a woven throw to use as a blanket. The pink one Layla had been left with had fallen victim to what Maddie kindly termed a "poopsplosion" while her uncle had been examining Layla. Linc had promptly turned green and produced a trash bag, seeming horrified that Maddie had been prepared to just toss the blanket in the washing machine. Instead, he'd promised to replace the blanket with a half-dozen if need be.

As for diapers and such, they had only what remained of the meager supply that had been left with Layla—also strongly depleted after the poopsplosion. Which meant Maddie was going to have to resupply. Soon. Because when it came to disposable diapers and formula, there was only so much improvising she was willing to do.

The second she picked up Layla, the baby stopped crying.

Her diaper still felt dry when Maddie checked, and

she cuddled her close. "You just want a little company, or are you hungry?" She turned the light on in the empty closet, leaving the door nearly closed so a little light seeped through, then sat down on the upholstered rocking chair in the corner and stood Layla on her thighs. The baby pushed down on her feet, bouncing jerkily. "I think it *is* just company you want. Don't you know that it's two in the morning, sweetie?"

The baby babbled and grabbed two handfuls of Maddie's hair, yanking merrily.

Maddie winced. "You need better toys than my hair," she murmured ruefully as she tried to disentangle herself.

"I'll take care of that tomorrow."

Startled, she looked over at the open doorway where Linc stood.

She might have gone to bed fully dressed, but Linc clearly had not. He wore only a pair of jeans. The rest of him above the waist was bare.

Gloriously bare.

She was glad for the dim light, because she was pretty sure if there'd been more, she wouldn't have been able to hide her gawking.

It *really* had been too long since she'd had a decent date if she couldn't keep from drooling over Lincoln Swift.

He stepped into the room and she quickly shifted her focus to the baby's grip on her hair. "A few plastic things from your kitchen would do just fine."

"Babies need stimulation. Your uncle talked about that when he was here."

"Yes, they do. Doesn't mean they need a bunch of fancy toys, though." Finally freeing herself, she quickly twisted her hair behind her neck with one hand and grabbed the baby's hands. "Oh no you don't, missy." She patted their hands together and Layla chortled, bouncing on her legs again. "They need love and attention. They need a safe environment and to feel secure."

"And health care and college funds."

She looked up at him. He'd crossed the room and was facing the oversize teddy bear.

She turned Layla around so she was sitting on Maddie's lap. "So what's going on between you and Jax?"

Except for the way the sinewy muscles roping over his shoulders flexed, he gave little response. "Nothing new. How do I get a DNA test done?"

Layla leaned her head back against Maddie's chest, and she couldn't resist rubbing her cheek against the infant's silky hair. "The hospital in Weaver can facilitate it. I know they've got a sizeable backload, though." His determination wasn't exactly a surprise, even though it had been more than a decade since she'd come up against it. "You *do* expect Jax to come back, don't you?"

Linc turned around, folding his arms across his wide chest. It only seemed to make his jeans hang even more precariously below some serious washboard abs. Maddie might be feeling her age lately, but Linc was five years older and, on him, thirty-five sat *very* well.

"He always comes back. He does own Magic Jax. Sooner or later, he checks in on the bar."

"And you really have no idea where he could be?"

He shook his head, then rubbed his hand over his chin, and then down his chest.

She chewed the inside of her cheek, trying not to stare. "You're going to look for him anyway. Right?"

His lips thinned. "I should have given you something to sleep in," he said, rather than answering her question.

Which just made her wonder even more about the

state of their brotherly love. "No need." It was much too easy to imagine slipping a T-shirt of Linc's over her head. And it wasn't professional at all. "It's one night. I'm fine like this."

"Have you slept at all?"

She nodded and stood. The spacious nursery felt much too close. "I think I'll fix Layla a small bottle. Maybe she'll sleep afterward. You want to hold her?"

He immediately shoved his hands in his front pockets.

She averted her eyes from the fine line of dark hair running downward from the flat indent of his navel, and headed toward the doorway. "I'll take that as a no."

"She's happy with you."

She realized he was following her, and hoped that he would turn into whichever room leading off the wide hallway belonged to him.

But he didn't. Soon, she'd reached the staircase. He flipped on a light as she grabbed the bannister and started down.

Since Maddie had first promised that she would at least stay there for the night, he hadn't made a single attempt to hold the baby. "You realize that if you *do* get your way where Layla is concerned—no matter how temporary—you're going to have to hold her. You're going to have to change a diaper or two. And you're not going to want to throw away every blanket just because it gets a little soiled."

"I'll cross that bridge when I come to it. Jax and I had nannies when we were little. So can Layla."

Sure. A single, male foster father. Who hired nannies. Judge Stokes would *love* that.

Maddie pressed her lips together and continued down the stairs in silence.

He flipped on lights as they made their way to the kitchen. The lone baby bottle was still sitting on a clean towel next to the sink where Maddie had left it last. Before she could mix up more formula, Linc did.

She sat on one of the bar stools at the island and watched.

And wondered some more.

About Linc and Jax.

About the nursery.

About how the bare skin stretching over Linc's shoulders would feel beneath her fingertips...

She swallowed and looked down into Layla's wide-awake face. The baby's fingers were again wrapped in Maddie's hair. Linc was warming the formula by holding the bottle under the faucet and running hot water the same way she'd done it. "From what I've heard, Swift Oil is doing well."

He made a sound. Agreement, she guessed. Although if Swift Oil weren't doing well, he wouldn't admit it. Greer would know. Her sister kept her finger far more securely on the pulse of local businesses than Maddie did.

Layla continued tugging merrily on Maddie's hair.

She noticed a crock of cooking utensils sitting next to the enormous gas range, so she got up and pulled an oversize wooden spoon from the selection. Layla released Maddie's hair and grabbed for it. Maddie returned to the stool, holding Layla on her lap. The wooden spoon smacked the counter and Layla jerked, gurgling. "Fun stuff, huh?"

Her eyes strayed to Lincoln's back, roving up the long, bisecting line of his spine. She was vaguely mesmerized by the shift of muscles.

But then she realized he'd shut off the water and was turning toward her, and felt her face start to flush.

Fortunately, he didn't seem to notice as he handed the bottle to her. "Hope it's warm enough."

She shook a few drops onto her inner wrist. "It's fine." The sight of the bottle had tempted Layla away from her banging. She quickly abandoned the spoon to reach for the bottle. Soon, her head was tilted back against Maddie's chest as she sighed and drank.

Something ached inside Maddie. Unless she ever met a guy who didn't stand her up, there wasn't any likelihood of answering that particular biological tick-tock anytime soon.

"Surprised you're not married by now with kids of your own."

Had he always been a mind reader?

She didn't look at him. "Could say the same about you. I'm sure you could have found someone good enough to take the illustrious Swift name." She shifted the baby's weight a little, almost missing the twisted grimace that came and went on his face. "What?"

He just shook his head before opening the refrigerator. "You want something to eat? Drink? Maybe a bottle of one of Jax's precious Belgian beers?" Linc glanced over his shoulder at her, holding up a dark bottle. "Suppose not," he answered before she could, and stuck the beer back on the shelf. "Milk is probably still more your speed."

She assumed that wasn't a compliment. "I don't need anything, thank you. And what's wrong with milk, anyway?"

"Not a thing." He pulled out a bottle of mineral water and let the door swing closed as he twisted off the cap. "If you're ten years old."

She made a face at him.

He sat down on one of the other bar stools. "Or nursing an ulcer."

"Speaking from experience?"

"So I've heard."

No doubt. He was more the type to cause them in someone else.

Despite everything, the thought felt uncharitable.

Layla's warm little body was growing heavier as she relaxed.

The only sounds in the kitchen came from the soft ticking of the clock on the wall and Layla's faint sighs as she worked the nipple.

Maddie swallowed. Her lips felt dry. She stared at the white veins in the dark gray soapstone counter, trying not to be so aware of him sitting only a few feet away. "Hard to believe it's going to be Christmas soon," she said, feeling a little desperate to say something. "The year's gone by really fast."

"Tends to do that the older you get."

She snuck a glance at his solemn profile. "You sound like your grandmother."

His lips kicked up before he lifted the green bottle to his mouth again.

"I remember the way she always decorated this place for Christmas." When Layla's head lolled a little, Maddie set aside the nearly empty bottle and lifted the baby to her shoulder to rub her back. Layla promptly burped and snuggled her face against Maddie's neck. "She always had the tallest Christmas trees. Tallest I'd ever seen, at least. Up until my grandmother, Vivian, moved to Weaver a little while ago from back East."

"We've met."

Maddie blinked but then dismissed her surprise.

Why wouldn't Vivian Archer Templeton—who was Richie Rich-rich thanks to Pennsylvania steel and a bunch of wealthy dead husbands—have met the guy who ran Swift Oil? "Anyway," she went on, "Vivian's tree was crazy tall the same way Ernestine's used to be. My grandmother's was more like an untouchable art piece, though. All covered in crystal and gold. What I remember about the trees here is that they were much homier." Popcorn garlands. Popsicle-stick ornaments. Real candy canes that Jax would sneak to school and share with Maddie and her sisters. "Her trees were like the ones my mother had. Only more than twice the size."

"My grandmother did love Christmas," Linc agreed. "I also think she was trying to make up for what Jax and I didn't have at home."

Maddie slid him a glance, surprised by the personal admission. "I must have been in junior high before I realized that you and Jax didn't actually live here all the time with her."

"Would have been easier if we had." He rested his forearms on the island and slowly rotated the water bottle with his long, blunt-edged fingertips. "She always dragged us to church when we stayed here." His hazel gaze drifted her way. "Could have done without being forced into a necktie for that."

She couldn't help smiling. "Jax always complained about having to wear a tie, too."

"Only good thing about going was knowing that Ernestine's pew was across the aisle from your folks' pew. Could watch the lot of you crammed between Meredith and Carter, wriggling and whispering and wanting to be anywhere else just as bad as me and Jax."

For some reason, his observation unnerved her.

"Church wasn't so bad." She still went most every week, after all. The church pew that his grandmother had always occupied was typically filled now by the mayor and his family.

She turned so that Linc would be able to see Layla's face. "Is she still awake?"

"Her eyes are closed. Looks asleep to me."

"Success." She carefully slid off the barstool. "And back to bed for everyone." She started to leave the room, but Linc didn't make any move to follow. "G'night."

"Night, Maddie."

A shiver danced down her spine.

She blamed it on a draft and quickly left the kitchen.

Even when she'd reached the top of the stairs, the light was still on in the kitchen.

For all she knew, he was often awake at two in the morning.

Which didn't matter to her one bit. Because she couldn't stand him, after all.

She padded silently down the hall and back into the nursery. Moving at a snail's pace lest Layla awaken, she gingerly lowered the baby back into the crib. And then she didn't breathe for what seemed another few minutes while she waited for Layla to stir.

When the baby just continued lying there, breathing softly, arms raised next to her head, fingers lightly curled into fists, Maddie finally exhaled. She leaned over the edge of the crib and gently covered Layla with the woven throw.

"Shoot for daylight next time," she whispered, before straightening and crossing to the closet to turn off the light.

Then she returned to her bedroom. There, she stretched

out on the bed once more and pulled the blanket across herself.

As tired as she was, though, all she did was stare into the dark.

Not thinking about her old friend Jax, and where he might be, or when he might return. And whether or not he really was Layla's father.

No. All she could think about was Linc.

And that dang shiver she'd felt when he'd said her name.

Both the females under his roof were still sleeping.

Linc finished silently closing the wooden blinds hanging in the window of the nursery. When the morning light was no longer shining through, he crossed the room, hesitating at the doorway into the adjoining room, even though he'd been determined not to.

He'd already glanced through the opening once.

Just long enough to see Maddie's long dark hair strewn across a white pillow.

An image that was going to be hell on him until he could banish it from his memory.

If he could banish it.

It didn't even matter that beneath the blanket, Maddie was fully dressed. The sight was still more tempting than any he'd seen in too long a time.

And, if she woke up and turned over, seeing him standing in the doorway leering at her, she'd grab up Layla and be out of there in a flash.

It was only that very real possibility that finally made him move away and leave the nursery altogether.

He didn't return to his own suite at the far end of the hall. He'd already showered and dressed for the day. He'd done it in record time, half expecting to hear Layla wailing at any moment.

But all had been peaceful in the nursery.

It was just inside his own head that everything was turbulent.

He usually spent most of his time at the office, even on the weekends. Swift Oil hadn't been the three-man operation Gus Swift had founded for a very long time. The company Linc had been entrusted with was now one of the major employers in the state. Certainly the major employer in Braden. The only company in the region rivaling his in terms of employment was Cee-Vid, located in Weaver. But not even Cee-Vid had the history of Swift Oil. The tech company hadn't been so much as a glimmer of thought when Gus Swift had first started out wildcatting with *his* father in the early 1900s.

When Linc wasn't working at the office, he was out working in the field. There was always something that needed doing, and when there wasn't, it meant there was something that needed undoing.

Something almost always caused by his and Jax's father, Blake. Blake, who was either diving into yet another inappropriate relationship, or planning another scheme guaranteed to cause Linc's ulcer to flare.

But that morning, the last thing on Linc's mind was the company. For the moment, anyway, Swift Oil was safe enough.

So instead of heading there, he went downstairs and into his home office. He'd plugged in his brother's dead cell phone the night before and when he picked it up and turned it on, he was rewarded by the familiar buzz that he got from his own phone.

But that was as far as he could go.

Because he didn't know his brother's password.

Knowing Jax, it could be anything from the name of his first girlfriend to the stock number of his favorite beer.

He sat down behind his desk, studying the cell phone screen. It bore a picture of a sailboat with a leggy blonde sunbathing on its deck.

Linc didn't know if the photo was some stock thing or from one of Jax's frequent escapades. For all Linc knew, the blonde could be Layla's mother. Though, admittedly, she didn't look to be in the family way. Even in the small picture, the minuscule bikini left nothing to the imagination.

He drummed the side of the phone a few times with his thumb. Then he abruptly swiped the screen and typed in "Maddie."

"Incorrect Password" flashed back at him before the sailboat returned to view.

He almost wished the attempt had been correct. He figured he could deal with his brother still carrying a torch for his high school girlfriend if it meant that Linc gained access to whatever secrets the phone might hold about Jax's present whereabouts. It wasn't as if Maddie was still likely to fall for Jax's charms. She was an adult now. Not a teenager who'd been too pretty, too soft-hearted and way too innocent for her own good.

Once upon a time he'd thought the same of Dana. And look where that had ended.

He quickly typed in "Dana."

The sailboat remained.

He pinched the bridge of his nose.

It ought to be too early for a headache.

"Linc?"

He dropped his hand and looked over to see Maddie standing barefoot in the doorway. Her hair was messy around her shoulders and her chocolate-colored eyes were dark and drowsy.

He couldn't stop the heat streaking through him any more now than he'd been able to when she'd still been a teenager and too damn young for him.

And it annoyed the hell out of him.

Jax may have slept with Dana. But Linc wasn't going to return the favor by poaching Maddie, no matter how attractive he found her. She wasn't too young for him now, but he still considered her off-limits. Not because of Jax. But because she was a decent woman. And the last woman who'd gotten involved with the Swifts and remained decent had been his grandmother.

His "What?" was more a bark than a question and her soft, drowsy eyes went cool.

She tugged down her sleeves. "I wanted to let you know that we'll be leaving now."

If his *what* had been terse, his "No!" was a flat-out command.

She lifted her eyebrows, unperturbed. "I'll let you know when the hearing is scheduled with Judge Stokes." She turned on her heel and disappeared from view.

He shoved away from his desk and went after her.

For a woman short enough to fit in his pocket, she moved fast, marching halfway up the stairs before he caught her arm. "Wait."

She looked pointedly at his hand on her arm and he released her. The second he did, she went up two more steps.

He caught her arm again. And this time, ignored her pointed glare. "I said, wait."

"So?" She yanked her arm free. "I'm not one of your oil minions, Lincoln. Layla needs diapers and formula. And I have things to do." She started to turn again, but stopped. "And don't suggest that I leave her here while I go and do them."

That had been the last thing on his mind.

He didn't want to let Layla out of his sight, but he still didn't welcome any notion that he'd have to take care of her *himself.* Not when the only thing he knew about caring for her had so far been learned from watching Maddie during the past eight hours.

"I'll pay you."

Her expression went from annoyance to fury to disgust. All in the blink of an eye. "Stooping to bribery isn't going to win any points, Linc."

Bribery? He nearly choked on the word. "I'm not bribing. I'm just willing to pay for your time. Why not? I pay for everyone else's."

"Well, not mine!" Her voice rose and her arms went out. "Get it through your head, Linc. For the next few days at least, Layla is under *my* care, by order of Judge Stokes. You started all of this by calling me in the first place. Now I'm going to do my job, whether you like it or not. The only thing *you* need to focus on is finding Jax!"

"I don't want you taking her out of the house."

"You're not calling the shots this time, so that's just too darn bad." She stomped up the rest of the stairs.

He followed her into the nursery where she scooped a very awake Layla out of the crib. "If you take her, I'm afraid you won't bring her back."

The admission didn't even make her hesitate. "You still keep talking as if *I* have some choice in the matter. Layla's immediate future is going to be determined by Judge Stokes." She carried Layla into the adjoining room. The bed looked pristine, as if Maddie's long thick hair had never spread across the white pillows at all.

"Even if I find Jax?"

"Even if you find Layla's mom!" She seemed to realize she couldn't put on her boots and hold the baby at the same time, but rather than try to hand the infant to him, she just set her in the middle of the bed before yanking on her socks. "I knew from the get-go that this was no safe-haven situation. Layla isn't a newborn, but even if she were, there would still have been protocols to follow when surrendering her. Appropriate places authorized to take a baby under those circumstances." She zipped her boots over her narrow jeans, right up to her knees. "Layla's too old. You heard my uncle. Considering her motor control and size, she's more likely three months than two. Parents don't get to just abandon their children on doorsteps without having some sort of reprisal. Layla's mother could walk in your front door right this minute and she wouldn't be allowed to bundle her up and truck on home with her! Even if she weren't guilty of abandonment, she is certainly guilty of neglect!"

"I don't give a damn about Layla's mother. As you're so fond of reminding me, she left her own baby on a freaking doorstep!"

Layla, apparently tired of their raised voices, got into the act, too, adding her own high-pitched wail.

Maddie gave him a now-look-what-you-did glare and scooped up the infant. "Like I said. She needs diapers and formula. So if you wouldn't mind moving out of our way, I'll go take care of those little requirements."

"I'll get you all the diapers and the formula you need. Just stay."

She lifted her chin. "You're free to buy whatever the heck you want, Linc. But I'm not staying. And I'm taking Layla with me. If you don't find Jax before the hearing, I can tell Judge Stokes that you've been helpful and supportive where the baby's welfare is concerned." She gave him a chilly, steady stare. "Or not."

So much for soft-hearted.

"Is this your version of hardball, Maddie?"

"Call it whatever you want." She didn't seem the least bit fazed as she brushed past him, carrying the baby in one arm and the car seat in the other. "It's the truth. You'll learn what everyone else learns sooner or later—don't piss off a social worker. It doesn't matter who you are or what you've achieved. We can be your best friend. And we can be your worst enemy."

He followed her back to the stairs. "You walked in the door last night already thinking of me as the enemy. You're still holding a grudge because I told you to stay away from Jax all those years ago."

She didn't even hesitate. "Don't give yourself so much credit, Linc. I don't think of you as the enemy. In fact, I really don't think of *you* at all."

Chapter Four

"*No.*" Ali was staring at her.

"You actually said that to him?" Greer was staring, too.

They were all sitting at the table in their eyesore of a kitchen. Layla—dressed in a diaper and nothing else—was lying on a blanket inside the portable play yard that Maddie had initially bought as a Christmas gift for her expectant sister and brother-in-law. The baby didn't need any clothes besides her diaper for the simple reason that the furnace in their house wouldn't shut off.

As a result, even though it was about thirty degrees outdoors, they were all dressed down to summer-weight clothes as befitted the overly toasty ninety degrees inside. Ali was even wearing a bikini top with her cutoff denim shorts.

"What else should I have said to him?" Maddie knew she sounded defensive, but couldn't help it. "Just because Lincoln Swift runs Swift Oil doesn't mean he runs everything else. He doesn't need to think he can run me."

"Don't you think you might be overreacting a little?"

Maddie glared at Greer. "Whose side are you on?"

Her sister lifted her hands peaceably. "Whose side are *you* on?"

"Layla's, obviously." She leaned over the side of the play yard and tickled the baby's tummy. Layla squealed and rolled partway onto her side, playing with her feet. "Who could leave such a darling like you that way?"

"Someone who was pretty desperate." Greer sipped her orange juice. She'd been working on case files when Maddie arrived, and a pencil was skewered through her hair, holding it off her perspiring neck.

"Maybe she had a furnace gone berserk, too," Ali said around the ice cube in her mouth. She was leaning back on two chair legs, her own bare feet propped on the corner of a sawhorse. "Lord knows it's making me feel pretty desperate. But I've gotta say, if a hot, manly-man like Lincoln Swift wanted me to stay a few nights under his roof, I'd be hard-pressed to say no." She raised a staying hand toward Maddie. "And I *know* he was supposedly awful to you back in the day, but the guy *is* hot."

"Supposedly?" Maddie made a face and refilled her own glass of juice from the pitcher Greer had set on the table.

"Even if Jax is Layla's daddy, she shouldn't have been left alone the way she was," Greer continued, as if Ali and Maddie hadn't spoken. "But it's all speculation until we learn more."

"I'm worried about Linc being able to find Jax any time soon," Maddie admitted.

"Did he say that?"

"He didn't have to. He doesn't know where Jax is. And he wants a DNA test to prove he's her uncle."

"Smart," Greer said. "In the absence of her parents, it would give him a positive legal stance. And you know it's a given that Judge Stokes will allow Layla to be tested considering the circumstances."

Layla let out a happy squawk when she managed to fit her toes into her mouth.

"On the up side in this whole thing, you *did* get to tell off Linc," Ali chimed in.

"I didn't tell him off." Not exactly. "He could have been a perfect stranger and I wouldn't have done anything differently."

Greer laughed softly. "So you'd have ignored your boss's vacation edict altogether *and* spent the night in a perfect stranger's house? Oh, Maude darling, I don't think so. You always did have a soft spot for both of those Swift boys."

Maddie gave Greer an annoyed look. "Don't call me *Maude*." She grabbed the paint chips from the table. "You two need to decide on paint, if we're going to get this room finished anytime soon."

Ali grabbed them back, shuffling them quickly. "I still want this one." She set the stack in the center of the table as if that decided the matter. "Too bad y'all were so careless handling the note left with the baby. I could have had it checked for fingerprints."

"Would only matter if Mommy Doe were already in the system. DNA's going to be the best bet." Greer picked up the chips and reshuffled. "And I still want this one. Where is the note, anyway?"

"Linc has it."

"The prosecutor's office is going to need it if they open an investigation."

"That's too dark. The kitchen'll feel like a cave." Ali quickly returned her paint choice to the top of the stack. "And we're all *assuming* that Mommy Doe was the one to dump Layla on the doorstep. What did the note say again?"

"Jaxie, please take care of Layla for me." The words felt tattooed in Maddie's mind. She took the paint chips and fanned through them. Greer wanted green. Ali wanted gray. There had to be a compromise they could all like. "I've dealt with a lot of strange situations, but this is one of the strangest." She flipped the paint chips around, leaving her choice on top. Svelte Sage.

"At least she's physically healthy," Greer murmured. She leaned over the edge of the play yard and offered Layla a finger. "You said Uncle David found no signs of malnourishment. No physical abuse."

"Thank God," Ali muttered.

"In fact, you're pretty perfect," Greer crooned, "aren't you, sweetheart?" Layla gurgled happily in response, which seemed to be all the prompting Maddie's sister needed to pick her up.

The second she did, though, she wrinkled her nose and handed the baby to Maddie. "Squishy diaper."

Maddie abandoned the paint chips for the baby. "Your fingers suddenly broken?"

"This is your job, hon. Not mine." Unperturbed, Greer sat back at the table. "Fun stuff like feeding her a bottle? Give me a call. Otherwise—" she waved her hand in a shooing motion "—she's all yours."

"Amen to that," Ali agreed.

Maddie grabbed a diaper from the package she'd picked up from the drugstore on the way home from

Linc's house, and took Layla into the living room where she could lay the baby on the couch. "What are the two of you going to do when Hayley's baby is born and you have to babysit?" Their half sister was five months pregnant with her first child. "It's just a wet diaper."

"Yeah, but you never know when a diaper is going to contain a surprise."

Maddie snorted, thinking of the massively messy diaper of the night before. "Trust me. This sweet girl gives you plenty of notice when that's the case."

She finished fastening the fresh diaper in place and balled up the wet one. A motion outside the window above the couch caught her eye and she watched a car pull up in front of the house. "Dad's here." She picked up the baby and carried her back into the kitchen, which—as hot as it was—was still the coolest spot in the house, thanks to the windows they'd opened.

"Thank God," Ali said fervently. "We can't afford a new furnace if Dad can't get this thing fixed for us. I'm tapped out for the next few months. I can't even afford to buy a new dress for Vivian's Christmas party this year. I wish she'd get over the black tie business. Got anything in your closets?"

"Don't look at me," Greer said. "Last thing you borrowed from me, you never returned. The only downside to asking Dad for help with the furnace is the number of times we're bound to hear 'I told you so.'"

None of them could argue that point. They all knew Carter considered the house his triplet daughters had purchased against his advice to be an absolute money pit.

Maddie threw away the wet diaper and put Layla back in the play yard, along with two brightly colored plastic cereal bowls from the cupboard. The baby immediately grabbed the red one and tried to fit it into her mouth. With the baby safely contained, Maddie washed her hands and went out to the living room where her sisters were already greeting their father.

"Hi, Daddy." She lifted her cheek for Carter Templeton's kiss when it was her turn. "Thanks for coming."

"Good thing you warned me," he returned, pulling off his jacket to reveal a short-sleeved T-shirt beneath. "Hot as a pistol in here."

"Which is why I'm hoping you brought your toolbox." Ali was looking pointedly at their father's empty hands.

"In the car. I know between the three of you, you can't seem to keep track of a hammer, much less a pipe wrench."

Ali whooped and immediately darted out the front door, not even stopping to get a sweater or shoes.

Carter just looked resigned. "How long's the furnace been running like this?"

Maddie led the way down the stairs to the basement. "It was running full blast when I got home this morning."

"This morning?" Carter's voice went tight with paternal overprotectiveness.

It didn't matter that she and her sisters were thirty years old. Carter took his fatherly duties very seriously.

"I had a case come up last night." Halfway down the stairs, she started feeling a little relief from the heat.

"A case." He sounded disbelieving. "Your mother told me you're on vacation for the next couple weeks."

She looked over her shoulder at him. "Some things interrupt a vacation, Dad. You know that better than anyone." He'd been an insurance agent and she couldn't recall a single time growing up when he hadn't dealt with one emergency call or another from one of his clients. "I'm taking care of an abandoned baby for a few days until we can get her situation resolved. Needless to say, it would be nice not to roast her out while she's staying with me."

"If I can't get this thing fixed, I'll have to get it cut off. Then you can start worrying about her freezing instead. What're you going to do for heat? You and your sisters will have to come home."

"This is home. I appreciate the offer—and I'm sure they would, too—but the fireplace is sound. We can manage if we need to." They may not be able to agree easily on paint color, but she knew her sisters would feel the same.

He made a grunting sound and moved past her when they reached the bottom of the stairs, heading toward the ancient furnace squatting like an antique behemoth in the middle of the room. "I warned you about buying a house with fifty-year-old plumbing and heating. But none of you would listen."

Ali had skipped down the stairs behind them. She set the toolbox on the cement floor, giving Maddie a wry look.

Carter bent down to open up his tools. "Go on," he said. "You know I hate someone watching over my shoulder."

It was a good enough excuse for both Maddie and Ali, and they retreated to the main floor, where they relocated the portable play yard to the living room. With Layla occupied with the colorful bowls, her fascinating toes and the monkey mobile hanging above the play yard, Maddie and Ali started unpacking the brand-new artificial Christmas tree.

More than an hour later, the furnace was still blasting

hot air. They'd opened up more windows, their father had gulped down a glass of tea and gone to the hardware store for a part, and she and Ali were still trying to decipher the instructions for the tree. Even Greer had taken a break from her case files to assess the situation.

Maddie was pretty sure the opportunity to feed Layla her bottle was the real draw, though. She'd had to use the last of the powdered formula to prepare it, which meant another trip to the store was imminent. She couldn't just swing by the corner drugstore where she'd gotten the diapers—the small spot on the shelf for formula had been cleaned out of product.

But at least the errand would give her a break from the hot house.

"I don't care what the diagrams look like." Ali tossed aside the single sheet of paper. "I'm telling you, we've got the whole bottom section upside down." She waved her hand with a flourish. "Just look at it!"

Maddie glanced toward their third sister. "What do *you* think?"

Greer barely looked up from Layla at the strangely box-shaped half tree. "I think this sweet girl is falling asleep on me." Her voice was soft. Crooning.

"I think someone's biological clock is ticking," Ali muttered sotto voce.

"Please," Greer said, obviously overhearing. "Speak for yourself."

"Trust me. I don't even own that clock," Ali assured her. She started dismantling the half-built tree. "Screw the directions. I'm starting over."

"We could have just had a live tree," Greer pointed out once Maddie took the sleeping baby and carefully transferred her back into the play yard. "It's a little more obvious whether they're upside down or not."

"Be glad we *don't* have a live tree," Ali retorted. She rebundled her hair in a messy knot and swiped her damp forehead with her arm. "It would be dried out in two days with the way the furnace is going full bore. You want to chance a fire—"

Greer lifted her hand. "Don't start. Sometimes you sound just like Dad."

Ali threw a tree branch at her head. Greer deflected it and propped her hands on her slender hips, studying the mess of tree branches tangled together with a rat's nest of tiny lights. "I thought these things were supposed to be easy to put together."

"All I know is that it was the one the sales guy recommended at Shop-World. And it was the best one of the few we could actually afford." Ali flipped over the base portion and managed to fit it back into the stand, but only by whacking it a few times with the heel of a boot. She straightened, stretching her back. "Okay." She waved at the branches littering the hardwood floor. "I've done my part. Rest is up to you."

"That means you," Greer told Maddie. "I've got to get those case files reviewed before Monday court. And it's just too hot to concentrate here. I'm going to head over to the office instead."

"You said you were going to help," Ali groused.

"And I will," Greer insisted. "*After* I get my work done."

"Well, *you* are going to decorate this sucker," Ali told her. "You got out of all the Christmas stuff last year, but if you try again, I'm going to hang wanted posters all over the branches."

"That'd be festive," Greer drawled. "I'll decorate, okay?"

"She better," Ali muttered as their sister left.

"She will," Maddie soothed. She would have accused Greer of shirking her Christmasy duty, too, if she weren't perfectly aware that their eldest triplet had a workload with the public defender's office that was completely insane. The fact that Greer had been home on a Saturday morning at all was unusual.

But Ali—as a police officer—was less tolerant of their third sister's career as a public defender.

So Maddie picked up a handful of the prickly branches without complaint and started fitting them in place under Ali's watchful eye.

They were still working on it when their father eventually returned, but neither paid him much attention as he came inside. "I suppose you're going to want me to fix that mess of a tree, too?"

"No," Ali drawled immediately. She was standing on a stepstool, fluffing out the upper tree branches. "And it's not a mess."

Maddie didn't look up. She was on her knees, her head wedged between the branches as she tried to locate the electrical plugs connecting all of the light strands together. She loved her dad. She really did. She didn't know what they would do without him. But sometimes, his attitude left a little to be desired.

Maybe their tree was a bit of a mess, but it was theirs.

"Thanks, though, Daddy," she added tactfully. "But you're already taking care of the sauna." She wrinkled her nose trying to alleviate a sudden itch. "That's a lot more important."

He made a "humph" sound full of doubt, but fortunately dropped it. All she could see of him through the tree were his shoes as he passed by. She finally felt the distinctive shape of the last plug and managed to thread the other cords through the branches until they met.

"I've finally got it, Ali." She stuck out her hand blindly. "Hand me the extension cord, will you?"

"Here."

The voice was deep. Definitely *not* her sister's, but recognizable anyway.

She let out a slow breath, taking the cord that Linc handed her and making the connection.

Then she extricated herself from the tree branches, giving Ali a withering look. Couldn't her sister at least have warned her?

But Ali had moved off the stepstool to sit on the couch. She was bouncing Layla on her lap, grinning like the Cheshire cat.

"I didn't know why your door would be open the way it was, so I came in to check." He took off his leather jacket. "Pretending you're in the tropics?"

Maddie swiped her tangled hair away from her cheek and scrambled to her feet, wishing like fury that she hadn't tied her ancient T-shirt in a knot under her breasts. With the paint-stained shorts she was wearing, she probably looked more like the seventeen-year-old he'd deemed unsuitable as a girlfriend for his brother than the responsible adult she really was.

"Furnace is on the fritz. What are you doing here? There was no need to check up on Layla." She gestured toward her sister and the baby. "As you can see, she's still with me. I haven't secreted her away to a foster family behind your back."

"I brought you supplies."

Only then did she realize the front door was still open and a pile of stuff was sitting right outside. A gigantic box of diapers. Three containers of formula powder. A case of ready-to-use formula bottles.

She didn't want to feel touched. Or concerned. But

she was—deeply. How was he going to react when things didn't go his way at the hearing? "You really didn't need to do all this." There was even a large box displaying a photo of an infant swing and a shopping bag bulging with heaven only knew what. "I hope you kept your receipts for when you end up returning most of it."

He just gave her a look.

Right. Lincoln Swift probably never returned anything.

"Your face is all red," he said.

"It's hot, as you've so tactfully observed." She folded her arms across her front, trying to hide the pale skin of her bare midriff. "My dad is working on getting the heat fixed."

"I ran into Carter outside. He told me."

She could just imagine. Her dad wasn't one to mince words, even in the best of circumstances.

Linc tossed his jacket aside. "And I meant your face is really red."

He was wearing the same gray pullover that he'd been wearing that morning. Cashmere, probably. With a thin line of white from his undershirt showing above the crew neck that had her thinking about what would be beneath *that*.

"Yeah." She rubbed her chin, hating the fact that he made her feel so self-conscious. And the fact that she knew what sort of body lurked beneath the cashmere. "I know. I'm a mess."

"No." Ali had unfolded her legs and stood. She stepped closer, carrying Layla. "Looks like you're getting a rash."

"Oh, for heaven's—" Maddie looked across the room toward the antique mirror hanging over the fireplace mantel. Her jaw dropped at her reflection, and she scrambled around the tree box and the play yard to get a closer look.

Her face was covered in red spots. And when she lifted her fingers to touch it, she realized the same splotches were springing out on her arms. And they were all suddenly itching as though a dozen ants were attacking.

In the mirror, she could see Linc lift Layla away from Ali. He held her awkwardly to one side, as if to shield her from whatever menace Maddie presented. The baby's legs dangled and she kicked them happily, as if it were some fun game. But it was a game that ended quickly when Linc laid her down inside her play yard. "What the hell have you exposed her to?"

"Nothing!" Maddie started rubbing her itching jaw and made herself stop. Her gaze fell on the tree. The damned prickly artificial Christmas tree that she'd been wrestling with for more than an hour. "It's that tree," she pointed accusingly.

"I don't know," Ali drawled. "Sure it's not mange?"

"Ali!"

Her sister laughed, spreading her hands. "I'm kidding!"

Maddie wanted to kick her. "Why aren't you breaking out in a rash?" They were identical sisters, for heaven's sake. If something about the tree was giving Maddie an allergic reaction, shouldn't it do the same with her sister?

Ali shrugged. "Clean living?" She tightened the messy knot on her head. If she felt the least self-conscious about her appearance around Linc, she hid it a lot better than Maddie did. "Go take a cool shower," she advised. "Maybe it'll help."

"Not if it's measles or something equally contagious," Linc said flatly.

"It's not measles!" Maddie could feel the situation escaping her control. "I've had all the shots I'm supposed to have. I am not sick, so stop hoping that I am."

"I'm not hoping anything." He stepped between Maddie and the baby, but he looked toward the front door as if measuring the distance. "I'm just being cautious."

"No, you're being ridiculous. And stop eyeing the door like that. I know what you're thinking, too. But you'd have to pick her up again to kidnap her."

His hazel eyes went hard. He looked incensed. "Kidnap. Do you always assume the worst, or is it just with me?"

Ali stepped between them. "Go take a shower," she said calmly to Maddie. "See if it helps. Linc isn't going anywhere. Are you, Linc?"

He looked like he wanted to argue. But maybe he had some respect for Ali's position as a cop, even though she was dressed like a sweaty beach bum. "For now," he said through his teeth.

Maddie met her sister's eyes. Linc had resources on top of resources at his disposal. And she'd seen desperate people do all sorts of desperate things they would never consider under ordinary circumstances. "I'll be just a few minutes," she warned.

"Take your time," Ali said easily. "It'll give Linc and me a chance to catch up." She sent Linc a winsome smile that made Maddie feel an unwarranted stab of jealousy. Ali had always been able to wrap men around her fingers with that smile. "Right, Linc?"

Chapter Five

"Good news." Her uncle David peeled off his sterile gloves and pitched them into the trash before flipping on the faucet to wash his hands. "Looks like a simple case of contact dermatitis." He turned back to Maddie where she was sitting on the examination table in his office.

After a shower had failed to bring her rash any relief, Linc had insisted she see a doctor. Then Carter had come up from the basement while she'd been arguing that Linc did *not* need to drive her to the hospital in Weaver, and had sided with him. Ali was the one to hurriedly suggest their uncle as an alternative.

Probably because she knew that Maddie had been about ready to lose her mind.

"Next time you touch your fake tree, wear long sleeves and gloves," her uncle advised, tilting her chin. "And try not to stick your face into it." He smiled. He was a few years older than her dad, and in general a much more easy-going guy. "Calamine and an antihistamine ought to take care of it. I'll prescribe something stronger if that doesn't give you some relief by tomorrow."

She hopped off the child-size table and tugged the hem of her sweater down around the blue jeans that she'd changed into. Even beneath the denim, her legs felt itchy. "Thanks. I appreciate you taking time for me. I was afraid I was going to get dragged to the hospital in Weaver whether I wanted to go or not."

"No problem. Had several patients today anyway. But a trip to the hospital seems a little extreme."

She was pretty sure nothing about her uncle's offices had changed since she'd been a child and he'd been her pediatrician. Even the painted cartoon characters circling the walls looked the same. "Would you do me a favor and tell Lincoln Swift that?" He was waiting for her in the waiting room. She hoped. "He's determined that I'm Typhoid Mary. Dad was almost as bad."

David chuckled as they walked back to the waiting room where his receptionist was cuddling Layla while Linc sat stiffly in one of the chairs. He was watching a trio of young children playing in the corner where a miniature table and chairs were situated. What he was thinking was anyone's guess. Maddie was just relieved to see that he hadn't bolted with the baby.

When she'd gone back to the examining room with her uncle, she'd tried to take the baby with her, but her uncle had intervened. She'd had no graceful way to get out of it, and had left the baby with Linc. Maddie doubted that he'd been the one to unbuckle Layla from her carrier. Which meant the receptionist had probably done it.

"I'm not contagious," she announced when he spotted her. "Sorry to disappoint you, but all I need is an antihistamine and a lot of calamine." She went to the receptionist to retrieve Layla, murmuring her thanks.

"She was fussing a little, so I took her out of the car seat," the woman said. "I hope you don't mind. I asked your husband, only he said he wasn't your husband." She was a young brunette Maddie didn't know, and she giggled a little as she went behind her desk. She was giving Linc an entirely appreciative look.

To his credit, he didn't seem to notice.

Maddie fit Layla back into the carrier that was sitting on the empty chair next to Linc. Before leaving the hot house, Maddie had dressed the baby once more in her polka-dotted sleeper. It was starting to look a little worse for wear. At the very least, Maddie would need to buy or borrow a change of clothes to get them through the next few days. But she wasn't going to say a word about it to Linc.

If she did, he'd show up with an entire winter wardrobe.

"Now that you know I'm not going to give some dreaded disease to Layla, you can drop us off at my house and head on your way." She hadn't wanted him to drive her, but she'd lost that argument, too.

"I spoke with Carter. He says your furnace is a lost cause. But he did get it disconnected. So the heat's off."

Her nerves tightened. Which was annoying in and of itself, because she was not usually the type to be so easily annoyed. "I would have found that out when I got home, but okay."

"He also said to tell you that your mom'll have your old beds made up for the night."

"And I'll tell him, again, the same thing I'll tell you. We'll be sleeping under my roof tonight, just like usual."

She yanked on the jacket she'd left in the waiting room and wrapped her fingers around Layla's seat handle, carrying it toward the door.

She tried hurrying ahead of Linc, but it was fruitless. He was at least a foot taller, and when his hand closed over the heavy carrier handle next to hers, she reluctantly let him take it from her.

She shoved her hands into her pockets. What was worse? Her skin tingling from that brief, disturbingly warm contact, or itching like fury?

While he set the car seat in the back of his enormous crew-cab pickup, he left it to her to buckle it in. She had to climb up inside the pickup to do it, and since she was already there, when she finished securing Layla she just buckled herself in beside her. "Home, James," she muttered under her breath while he rounded the pickup to get behind the wheel.

"Say something?" His eyes found hers in the rear-view mirror as he started the engine.

She shook her head and tucked her itching hands beneath her thighs. If she bathed in a vat of calamine, perhaps she could avoid taking an antihistamine. They always made her feel exhausted.

"It's supposed to snow tonight."

She shifted, pressing her thighs a little harder against her hands. It wasn't as good as the forbidden scratching— but it was better than nothing. "Well. It's mid-December. Snow happens."

"Temperature's supposed to drop another twenty."

"I appreciate the weather report, Linc." She dragged her hands free and rubbed the back of them against her ribs. If he didn't get moving soon, she was afraid she'd beg him to make a stop so she could stock up on a gallon or two of calamine. Because she was pretty sure the bottle in her medicine cabinet wasn't going to cut it. "Could we, uh, get going please? Layla needs a diaper change." It was an outright lie, but she figured a forgivable one given the circumstances.

He stretched his arm across the seat as he looked back at her. "You're not going to have any heat," he said with the patience of one speaking to a nitwit. "Your furnace is disconnected."

She grimaced. "You and my father ought to form a club. The house was over ninety degrees when we left it. And we had windows open! It's not going to cool off that fast. We're not going to freeze in our sleep. Layla will be *fine*." Oblivious to being the topic of conversation, the baby's eyelids were beginning to droop. Layla was like nearly every baby ever: a running car engine inspired her to catnap.

Linc's lips compressed. He turned around to face the front and put the truck into gear. "You're more stubborn than you used to be."

"Yeah, well, I'm not seventeen anymore."

He made a sound. "Trust me. I've noticed."

She flushed. He didn't make it sound like a compliment.

"What I'm getting at is obvious," he continued. "*I* have a furnace that operates properly."

"And I have firewood and a fireplace. I'm not bringing Layla back to your house."

"Until the judge says so."

She pressed her knuckles against her ribs, rubbing in circles, and sighed. "I don't know how many times I need to warn you how unlikely that is. At least until we know more about Layla."

"Everyone thought it was unlikely my grandfather would strike oil, too."

She looked out the windshield. In the distance, she could see the oil derrick that stood like a metal monolith on the horizon. Every school kid in Braden grew up hearing the story of Swift Oil's first successful oil strike. That discovery well was no longer active, but only because it didn't need to be. The home office of Swift Oil was still located in Braden—a tribute to its humble beginnings, or so the advertising went—but there were three other offices spread around the state, dealing in everything from crude oil to natural gas to alternative energy.

Yet for all of Gus Swift's early success in the oil business, it had never seemed to Maddie that the man's family had ever benefitted all that much. Ernestine had been widowed when her only son, Blake, was still young. She'd never married again, and Blake turned out a jerk. She'd done more to raise her grandsons when they'd come along than their parents had.

"Does your dad still have a hand in running Swift Oil?"

"Why?" The single word held a wealth of suspicion.

She let out a huff. "I don't know! Do you have to be so touchy? I'm just making conversation and trying not to scratch! I've never had poison ivy, but I bet this is worse."

He braked at a stop sign and looked over his shoulder at her again. "It's not worse than poison ivy. I had it when I was a kid. Your face isn't even all that red anymore. And I'm not touchy."

She raised her eyebrows. "O...kay."

His jaw canted to one side. But then he turned to face the wheel once more and continued driving. "I contacted one of my lawyers while you were in with the doc."

"And?"

"He specializes in mineral rights. He referred me to someone else who deals in family law."

She knew all the attorneys in the area who handled anything remotely regarding family law. There were only a few, including her brother. "That's good. Who?"

"Tom Hook. Over in Weaver. He's setting up the DNA testing. So it will all be official, in case I need to use the results in court."

"Tom's a good guy." A rancher as well as a lawyer, the older man had a sensible approach to things that Maddie generally appreciated. "He handled a custody case I was involved with a few years ago."

"You're not going to argue about it with me?"

She couldn't help groaning as she wriggled in the seat, rubbing her itching back against the leather upholstery behind her. "Just because I'm following the rules about Layla's immediate status doesn't mean I'm hoping you're *not* her uncle. For her sake, I mean. Get that established and things are much simpler. Until Jax returns or we find Layla's mother or another close family member, you'll have every right to request she be placed in your care. Until then, or if the test is negative—"

"It won't be."

She ignored that. "Then shelter care is still necessary. Did Tom give you any idea when the test would be scheduled?" If genetic testing was conducted for legal reasons, there were certain stipulations that had to be followed. The entire process was witnessed. Strictly controlled and documented.

"He's getting back to me on it."

He turned down another street and they passed Magic Jax, the bar his brother owned. "Have you talked to any of Jax's workers at the bar? Seen if anyone there knows how to reach him?"

"The manager."

"And?"

"He's new. Didn't even know Jax had left town. But then the guy doesn't strike me as the sharpest crayon in the box."

"What about the servers?" The last time she was in the bar—admittedly quite some time ago—all of the servers had been female. Comely ones. Jax liked comely women.

He shook his head. "I just spoke with the manager this morning. Bar doesn't open until later this afternoon."

She studied the back of Linc's head. His thick hair was a little long at the neck. A little wavy at the ends. At his grandmother's funeral, it had been rigidly short.

"Is that scratching I hear?"

She immediately flattened her fingers against her thighs, holding them still. Beneath the denim, her skin felt on fire. "No."

"You always were a bad liar."

She made a face at the back of his head. Childish? Yes. But also satisfying. "Unlike you, who *always* spoke the truth. As you saw it, anyway."

He made another turn. "We're back to that? Are you ever going to get over it? It was a decade ago."

"Thirteen years." The words escaped before she could stop them.

"Fine. *Thirteen* years ago. You and Jax weren't suited. I'm sure your parents thought the same thing."

Her dad had been full of dire warnings about Jax's reputation. Her mother had been less concerned; she'd understood that Maddie and Jax were just buddies. Of course, Meredith had once caught Maddie doodling *Mrs. Lincoln Swift* all over her notebook, too.

His eyes caught hers in the rearview mirror again. "Are you going to sit there and say you've been nursing a broken heart for Jax ever since? What's been stopping you? I've been gone for more than half that time."

"That's not the point."

He gave a disbelieving snort. "He'd have broken your heart long before now if I hadn't stopped things before they went too far. And you have to know it, too, by now."

It was her turn to snort. "As if that was your concern. You just didn't want Jax being serious about *me*. My mother had cleaned house for your grandmother. We weren't country club folk."

"Country club folk!" They'd reached her house and he pulled up to the curb, stopping so hard that she jerked forward. He looked back at her again. "What the hell is that supposed to mean? Braden doesn't even have a country club. Not then. Not now."

"No, but there were still differences between your family and mine. You got back from graduating college and decided I wasn't good enough for your family and that was that!"

"It wasn't you who wasn't good enough. Even as a teenager, Jax was a chip off our old man. I didn't want him putting *you* through the wringer."

Layla whimpered and Maddie automatically stroked her soft little arm, soothing her. "Please. You'd been off to college for four years. At that point, I bet I knew Jax better than you did. He wasn't going to put me through any wringer!"

"Well, if you thought he'd put a *ring* on your finger, you were going to be disappointed. Jax still doesn't know how to commit to anyone. And he doesn't give a damn who gets hurt in the process."

"Oh, for Pete's sake! I was seventeen. I didn't want a ring. Pretty much all I wanted was a date to prom!" She shoved open her door and hopped out, intending to go around and unbuckle Layla from the other side, but Linc beat her to it.

"Just go inside and take care of yourself," he said when she hovered near his side while he struggled to release the car seat. "I'm not going to steal her, for Christ's sake."

She supposed she deserved that.

She turned and headed toward the house, scrubbing her palms down her legs as she went. The front door was closed, which she took as a good sign. When she went inside, though, it was only marginally cooler.

All of the supplies that Linc had brought earlier had been moved inside and stacked on the couch, covering nearly every inch.

The Christmas tree had been pushed into one corner of the living room. Even though Maddie had to admit that it was a nicely shaped tree—now that it was put together properly—she had no desire to go near it ever again. If it were going to have more decoration on the green branches than a few hundred tiny white lights, Greer would have to hold up her end of things.

Beyond that, there was no sign of Ali or her dad.

Linc came in, holding the carrier in front of him as if it was a bomb in danger of going off. "She's still asleep," he whispered.

"Congratulations. Set her carrier in that chair." She pointed to one of the armchairs near the couch. "She'll be fine there for a while."

He did as she asked, then stood back, hands on his hips as he studied the room.

She looked at it through his eyes. The furniture was straight out of the eighties. A shag rug equally mismatched to the Victorian architecture partially covered the parquet wood floor, not even remotely hiding all of the boards needing repair. "What's wrong, now?"

He just shook his head and silently moved the armchair until it was butted up against the other chair, effectively walling in the car carrier. "Now there's no way she can fall out." He was still whispering, even though Maddie hadn't.

She bit the inside of her cheek. The car seat harness still buckled around Layla would have done the trick, but oddly, Maddie didn't have the heart to point it out to him. Or address the fact that the play yard that was pushed against the wall doubled quite well as a crib.

Instead, she waved at the couch. "You really overdid it with the supplies. But thank you. It was very generous." She pressed her fingertips against her chin, trying not to scratch.

He pulled off his jacket and tossed it on top of the gigantic box of diapers. "Where do you want the swing?"

She raised her eyebrows. "To stay in the box?"

In answer, he pulled a folding knife from his pocket and silently began slicing open the tape holding the box closed.

She exhaled. He clearly had no intention of leaving yet. "You are way too used to getting your way."

"Shh. You'll wake her up." Finished with the tape, he pocketed the knife again and folded open the box flaps. "And when I can get what I want, why not?" He began extracting the swing parts. "So, where do you want it?"

Since the coffee table was the only place left in the

room to sit, she sat down on the edge of it and tucked her hands under her thighs again. "I guess where the chair used to be before you fashioned it into a crib."

He set the white-painted metal legs on the marks left in the rug by the chair and reached back into the box. "Find me a screwdriver, and then go take something before you scratch holes through your jeans."

"I'm not scratching."

He just gave her a look.

She got up and went into the kitchen where she hoped she would find a screwdriver lurking in one of the drawers. Her father hadn't been exaggerating when he'd complained about their ability to keep hold of simple tools. For whatever reason, they kept disappearing, only to turn up in the strangest places.

Maddie blamed it on Greer. Greer blamed it on Ali. Ali blamed it on ghosts.

There was no screwdriver. Not in the drawers. Not on top of the refrigerator. Not inside the old-fashioned metal breadbox, even though Maddie had found a hammer there once.

She went back into the living room.

Layla was stirring, making sounds, but not yet opening her eyes. Linc was sitting on the floor, surrounded by infant swing parts. The directions—looking considerably more detailed than the Christmas tree instructions—were lying on the floor, but he didn't seem to be giving them any attention. "I can't find a screwdriver," she admitted.

"You can't be a homeowner without basic tools."

"You sound like you went to the school of Carter Templeton." She spread her hands. "What can I say? Blame the ghosts. Ali does."

He pulled out his pocketknife again. "Ghosts?"

"It's just something she says." Heaven forbid he take

that seriously. She could just imagine him in front of the judge. *Your honor, she thinks her house has ghosts...* "We don't have ghosts."

"Glad to hear it. Did you at least take something for your rash while you were crashing around in the kitchen?"

"I wasn't crashing around."

"Enough to wake up Layla."

Maddie glanced again at the baby. Still no opened eyes. "I didn't wake her up." But she hadn't gotten to the medicine cabinet yet, so she left the room again, heading upstairs.

She found the bottle of calamine lotion without a problem. But the contents were separating and when she checked the expiration date, she could see why. She dropped the bottle in the trash and grabbed the box of antihistamine tablets, reluctantly swallowing a dose before going back downstairs.

This time, Layla's eyes were open.

Maddie stepped around Linc, who was impersonating MacGyver by using his pocketknife as a screwdriver, and unfastened the harness straps so she could lift the baby out of the car seat. "Hello, sweet pea."

Layla screwed up her face and let out a lusty wail.

Linc frowned accusingly. "What are you doing to her?"

"Pinching her, of course," Maddie deadpanned. "I'm sure she's hungry." She plucked one of the ready-to-use bottles from the case he'd brought and went into the kitchen. They still had only the one nipple. She quickly prepared the bottle and laughed softly when Layla grabbed for it, her wailing ceasing the second she got her mouth around the nipple.

With Layla happily gorging herself, they returned

to the living room once more. Maddie nudged one of the chairs away from its "crib" mate enough so that she could sit down with the baby in her lap.

She watched Linc for a moment. He had the legs of the swing assembled and was working on putting together the seat. The direction sheet was now shoved halfway beneath the coffee table.

"You seem pretty adept at that."

He didn't look up. "Putting a few parts together— it's not rocket science."

"Or a Christmas tree," she murmured. She watched Layla's blissful face for a few moments. "Why did your grandmother put in a nursery?"

Chapter Six

Why did your grandmother put in a nursery?

Maddie's question circled inside Linc's head while he popped the seat into the motor assembly. He wondered if she already knew the answer. Or at least suspected. But if she did, she was better at hiding her thoughts than he'd given her credit for.

Either way, he might as well tell her. There were plenty of other people who knew.

Jax, for one. Not only had Dana cheated on Linc with him, it turned out she'd been cheating on Jax, as well.

"Because my wife was pregnant." Using the dinky screwdriver attachment on his knife, he tightened the seat.

He finally glanced at Maddie when her silence lasted longer than usual.

She was staring at him, her soft lips parted. "You have a child?"

"No." He connected the swing legs and tightened a few more screws. Nor did his wife, since she had chosen to end the pregnancy.

Maddie was still staring. "I've never heard you're married. You don't wear a ring."

"That's because I took it off when I stopped being married. It was a long time ago."

"How long?"

He wished he'd kept his mouth shut. "Six years." He flipped the swing right-side up and eyed the last part. It was a mobile meant to be hung from the housing above the seat. He unfurled the tightly wound purple and pink horses and threaded it into place. "I thought babies liked bunnies and bears and little baby stuff."

"Sorry?"

He flipped his hand across the mobile, making it swing. "These are horses."

"Unicorns." Still holding Layla, Maddie slid off the chair onto her knees and came closer. With her free hand, she stilled one of the dangling unicorns. "There's the silver horn. It's just a little bent, but the fabric will straighten out in time." She stilled another. "This is a Pegasus. You'll have to know these things with a little girl around. It's all unicorns and a flying Pegasus at first. Until she gets a little older and then, like with me, it *is* all horses. Real ones. I always wanted one, but the closest I ever got to any was at your grandmother's."

Her lashes lifted and he got a blast of her warm, chocolate eyes.

She blinked once and looked back at the mobile. "She had three. Laughy, Taffy and Daffy. Taffy was always the first one to get to the apples we'd feed her." She gave him a self-deprecating smile. "You don't need me to tell you about *your* grandmother's horses."

Nor about Maddie and her sisters feeding them apples. Carrots. Whatever they could get their enthusiastic little hands on.

He remembered all right.

But he made a face and pushed to his feet. He'd do what was right where his brother's child was concerned. But he didn't want to sit there feeling this churning inside. He already had one barely healed ulcer. He didn't want another.

"Call me when you come to your senses and are ready to stay at my house," he said abruptly. "I'll send someone to pick up all the gear so you don't have to drag it along with you and the baby."

The soft look that had been in her eyes disappeared. She focused on the baby in her arms as she moved back to the chair. "I'll call you when I know when the hearing is scheduled," she corrected.

He made himself shrug. As a little girl, she'd been shy and eager to please. As a teen, she'd been wide-eyed and innocent, no matter what she claimed about his brother and the prom. As a woman, he was quickly learning there was no point in arguing with her. He'd have to trust that she'd come to her senses soon enough. "Call me if you need anything else."

She gave a pointed look at the swing and the supplies covering the couch. "I think Layla is set for quite some time."

"And you?" Instead of heading to the door the way he should have, he crossed to her and lightly caught her chin, nudging it upward. She still had a splotch of red on her right cheek and a slightly smaller patch on her chest, right above the scooped neckline of her ivory sweater. Layla's head was lolling against Maddie's chest as she ate, causing the sweater to dip even more, giving

Linc an excellent view of smooth, pale skin cupped by creamy white lace.

Not that he looked.

Layla's big blue eyes were staring up at him, looking almost glazed. She didn't even blink as she drank.

Ernestine had never blinked when she was ferreting some truth out of him, either.

So maybe he looked. For a second.

Shoot him. He wasn't dead.

He let go of Maddie's chin. "Are you set, too?"

Her pupils seemed to dilate. The splotch on her cheek became less noticeable because the rest of her face turned pink. "For what?" Her voice sounded a little faint. Then her lashes lowered. She gave a quick cough. "I mean, I'm fine, too. I think the, um, the antihistamine is starting to kick in already."

"The itching better?"

She shook her head and a lock of long brown hair slid over her shoulder. "Starting to want a nap. Stuff always makes me sleepy. That's why I hate taking it."

Layla had one little dimpled hand spread against the side of the bottle, looking as if nothing else on earth existed but that bottle. But the second she spotted Maddie's hair, she wound her other hand around it. Her eyelids finally drooped to half-mast.

"You're not the only one wanting a nap."

Maddie looked down at the baby. The pink was fading from her face and her expression turned tender. She tugged the bottle away and dabbed a drop of formula from the baby's chin. "Looks like milk coma to me." She set aside the bottle before pushing to her feet. Then she carried Layla over to the play area and gingerly lowered her down into it. Layla gurgled a few times and threw her hands out wide, then gave a soft snore.

Maddie straightened and pressed her hands to the small of her back, arching.

"That's why you need to use a crib," Linc pointed out. "Saves your back. You don't have to reach so far down for the baby."

Her lips twitched. "Nice try." She started to scratch her chest, but curled her fingers into a fist and headed toward the door instead. She yawned before she even got it open.

"Who's going to watch the baby while you sleep? You're the only one here."

"You're joking, right? Moms have been sneaking naps along with their babies since the dawn of time. I may not be a mom, but I figure it's still a good plan."

She swung the door open even wider and the cold air was almost a relief. Because it was still way too warm in the house.

"I'd better stay."

She handed him his jacket, then shoved at his shoulders. "You'd be a lot more useful tracking down Jax." She seemed to realize that he hadn't progressed an inch out the door, and snatched her hands back. "Go to Magic Jax. Talk to Jax's waitresses in person. See if they know anything."

She was right. He'd planned to do all of that. But plans seemed to have a way of changing whenever Maddie was around. "Don't forget to put some of that pink stuff on your rash."

She pressed her palm against her belly and dropped it immediately.

Considering how she'd had her T-shirt tied up underneath her breasts when she'd been hanging half in, half out of the Christmas tree, he could only imagine how irritated the rest of her torso was. "I'd offer to help with the hard-to-reach spots, but you'd probably take it the wrong way. Wouldn't want to be accused of bribery again."

"Wouldn't matter anyway, since we're out of calamine. And you can joke if you want about bribery, but there have been attempts. More than once and not just with me." She leaned against the door. Her eyes were looking drowsier by the second. "Generally the situations that land families in my office are the kind of situations that cause desperation. And desperation is a powerful motivator for people to do the kind of unreasonable things they'd never ordinarily consider."

"I'm not desperate enough to do anything stupid."

Her smooth brow wrinkled. "You were desperate enough to call me last night for help."

"Yes, but that wasn't stupid." Not for any of the reasons she seemed to think, at least. "Go take your nap with Layla. I'll be in touch."

She nodded, but stood in the open doorway watching him until he got in his truck. Only then did she finally close the door, and he drove away.

Since he was in the area, he stopped first at Magic Jax. It wasn't quite time for the bar to open but there were a few cars parked in the lot, so he went around back and pounded on the locked service door until it opened.

Even though it had been years since Linc stepped foot in the place, he still recognized Sal Romano's face. The bouncer had been with Jax longer than anyone else his brother had ever hired. Maybe because they were friends from way back.

The burly man grinned, showing off his two front teeth capped in gold. His long hair had more gray than red and was held back in a scraggly ponytail. "Damn!

Hell must have frozen over." He stuck out a beefy hand. "How you doing, Linc?"

Linc's palm was swallowed in the other man's handshake. "It's been a while."

Sal chuckled. "Long enough for both of us to be looking grayer, anyway." He stepped back so Linc could enter the building. "What brings you by? Finally checking up on your investment?"

There weren't too many people who knew that Linc had staked his brother enough to start up the bar nearly seven years ago. And nobody but Linc knew that he'd stupidly done so at the behest of his then-wife. The only solace to that was knowing that Dana had been faithless to Jax, too.

"Checking up on my brother, more like." He followed the bouncer around the crates waiting to be unpacked in the stockroom and into the small business office. "Don't suppose you've heard from him lately?"

"Nah." Sal sat on the edge of a scarred, metal desk. "But you know Jax. He gets a wild hair about something and off he goes. Chasing snow. Chasing waves." Sal scratched the rattlesnake tattoo climbing up his forearm. "You're not worried about him, are you?"

Worried? No. Furious? Yes. Still, Linc shook his head. "Just have some stuff we need to deal with."

"Swifty stuff." Sal nodded sagely. "I'll bet."

Linc didn't bother to correct him. Aside from Jax's shares in the family business, his brother had little interest in the running of it. And that was fine, until recently, when Linc needed Jax to vote with him against their father's proposal to sell the company outright to an outfit based in Oklahoma.

But Jax had left town first, leaving Linc on his own to try to talk reason into his dad. Typically, Blake was more concerned with lining his own pockets than he was with the fact that selling their company to OKF meant they'd also be selling out their employees.

As a result, Linc had been forced to go straight to OKF to kill the deal.

He still wasn't entirely sure he'd succeeded.

"Jax talk to you a lot about the company?"

Sal laughed again and shook his head. He picked up a clipboard that was thick with papers curling up at the edges and flipped through them. "Just enough so that I know he enjoys the perks that come with it. Telling the ladies he owns a bar is one thing. Telling them he's one of the owners of an independent oil company? Well, you know how that is. Tends to net him a whole different class of lady."

"Any ladies in particular?"

Sal stopped flipping pages and signed the top sheet, then dropped the clipboard back onto the desk. His smile faded. "You wanting to know if he had a particular woman when he went off this time?"

If Jax did have a woman with him, it wouldn't have been Layla's mother. What would have been the point of leaving Layla the way she had? Why would the note be meant for him, when he wasn't even there? Still, any information was better than no information. "Did he?"

Sal's expression turned sober. "I don't know for sure. But I know who was coming around before he left. You're not going to like who it was."

Linc exhaled, knowing instinctively what the other man was going to say. He'd successfully escaped his ex-wife. But Jax had never seemed able to do the same. "Dana, I suppose."

He nodded. "Sorry, man. Gotta suck knowing your own brother's—uh, seeing your ex-wife."

All things being relative, Linc could name a few other things that ranked just as high on the suck-o-meter. "Any women come in here yesterday specifically looking for him?"

"Hell, Linc." The bouncer's expression turned wry. "Half o' Jax's customers are women coming in here specifically trying to meet him. Think it's one of the reasons why he's hardly ever here anymore. There's such a thing as too much of a good thing."

"What about the last year? Anyone seem particularly involved with him besides Dana?" He knew his ex-wife couldn't be Layla's mother. He'd have recognized her handwriting on the note, for one thing. And for another, he'd run into her about six months ago when he'd been in Cheyenne on business. She definitely had not been pregnant.

"No more than usual." Sal's eyes narrowed. "What're you really trying to find out?"

Linc sighed. Word was going to get out soon enough about the baby, he supposed. "Someone left a baby with me last night."

The bouncer looked stunned. "Jax's baby?"

Even though he had a sudden image of Maddie shaking her head and cautioning him about his conclusion, Linc nodded. "That's my thinking, anyway."

"Well, damn." The other man spread his palms. "Sorry I'm not more help."

"Don't worry about it." At least Sal had been more enlightening about Jax than the bar manager. "You need to be the one managing this place."

Sal just shook his head. "Then I'd have to do all that hiring and firing. Those cocktail waitresses we've got? Constantly coming and going. Don't have a single one who has been here more than half a year. But look. If

I hear anything about your brother, I'll let you know." He shrugged. "He never stays gone more than two or three weeks at a stretch. Christmas coming? He'll be back in time for that. Always busy here at the bar during the holidays."

"Thanks, Sal."

"You bet. A couple of the girls ought to be coming on shift by now. Maybe they know more than I do."

Linc wasn't going to hold his breath. Still, he went out through the front where a skinny girl was twining silver and red garland around a Christmas tree that looked very similar to the one Maddie and her sisters had put up. Not surprisingly, neither she nor her co-worker gave him any useful information and he left.

Before finally heading to his office, though, he stopped at a drugstore and bought a couple large bottles of calamine lotion. Then he drove back to Maddie's house. The front door wasn't propped open this time, but it was nevertheless unlocked.

Annoyed, he silently pushed it open.

In the living room, Layla was still sleeping flat on her back. Maddie had moved all the stuff off the couch and was sprawled on it, also flat on her back. It was a toss-up as to who was sleeping more soundly.

He stood there, watching both of them.

After a few minutes, though, he made himself move.

He carried the containers of formula into the kitchen, shaking his head over its deplorable state. It was obvious that she and her sisters were trying to renovate the room, but equally obvious that they were nowhere near completion.

He was tempted to explore the rest of the house and see if it was in an equally unfinished state. The living room hadn't been so bad. Besides the serviceable furniture that he'd bet they'd gotten secondhand, the wood floor had shown signs of its age. But the fireplace looked sound enough. At least from the outside.

If she was going to insist on staying there—and needing to use the thing—he'd make sure the chimney was cleaned.

The packing materials from the infant swing were still on the floor, so he gathered it all up, stuffing it back in the oversize box and leaving it in the screened-in porch at the back of the house. He'd haul it away later if she wanted.

He set the bottles of calamine lotion on the coffee table where Maddie was sure to see them when she woke and, on the back of the swing's instructions, wrote a note that he propped against the bottles.

Then he crouched next to the net siding of the play yard. He watched the baby's little chest rise and fall. "See you soon, Layla," he whispered.

She slept on.

He pushed to his feet and left.

Stop leaving your doors unlocked.

Maddie sighed and folded the paper until Linc's note no longer showed. She ran her fingers along the edges as she looked at the bottles of calamine.

It was entirely unnerving to know that he'd come into the house while she slept.

"He could have been anyone coming inside," she said to Greer. It was only her sister returning to the house that had woken up Maddie. Layla had already been awake, gurgling nonsense to herself as she played with her plastic cereal bowls.

"In Braden?" Greer raised her eyebrows. "I sort of doubt it."

"Crime happens here, too. If it didn't, you wouldn't have a job as a public defender. Ali wouldn't have a job as a police officer."

"Point taken. But we don't have home invasions," Greer amended.

"What if he'd taken Layla?"

"He didn't." Her sister gestured toward the calamine. "He didn't take away. He delivered. I think it was pretty sweet of him, actually."

Maddie made a humming sound. She wanted to disagree. But couldn't.

"In fact, I'm definitely getting the sense that Lincoln Swift doesn't disapprove of you quite as much as you always said."

Maddie pushed her disheveled hair behind her ears. "I never said he disapproved of me. He just didn't think I was good enough to date Jax."

"Well." Greer still didn't look convinced. "Linc definitely has a protective streak. I mean, look around."

Maddie chewed the inside of her cheek. "He *says* he only warned me away from Jax for my own protection."

"Hmm." Greer nodded slowly. "I could see that, considering the family history. Blake Swift is notorious for cheating on his wife."

"Jax and I were kids! We weren't destined for marriage. We weren't destined for anything. He was just fun to be around."

"True. Although, I always thought Linc was more interesting than Jax."

He was.

He is.

Maddie rubbed her finger against the dull throb behind her forehead. Darned antihistamines. "Really? I never thought about it," she lied. Then she ruined it all. "Did you know that he'd been married?"

Greer looked surprised. "Should I have? You're the one who had a crush on him."

"I did not!"

"How'd you find out?" Greer leaned forward, her eyes sly. "Tender confidences?"

"You read too many romance novels."

Her sister snorted. "I read legal briefs and professional journals. And I think you're being evasive."

"It's no big deal," Maddie said defensively. "It just came up in conversation."

Greer gave her a knowing look. "Must have been some conversation."

She wished she'd kept her mouth shut and changed the subject entirely. "Did you finish all your lawyerly homework?"

"Almost. A few hours tomorrow and I should be set for court on Monday."

"Good. The tree still needs decorating. And *I'm* not going to do it."

"Since you still have a rash on your face, I suppose that's fair." Greer nudged one of the calamine bottles closer to Maddie. "He clearly bought it for you to use."

Maddie hesitated. She didn't know why she was so reluctant. But she'd spent so many years thinking the worst about Lincoln Swift. Seeing him this way—so intent on Layla, who may or may not be his niece—was messing with her mind.

Obviously.

"Come on, Maude," Greer chided. "No time like the present."

"I should check Layla's diaper." The baby was trying to fit her entire fist into her mouth. The fact that she was also holding on to one of the plastic cereal bowls at the same time only added to the challenge.

"Yeah, she looks positively miserable." Greer handed Maddie one of the bottles of lotion.

"Oh, fine." Maddie snatched it out of her sister's hand. "But only if *you* change Layla's diaper."

"I don't do diapers and all that baby stuff, remember?"

Maddie made a face at her. But since that face still felt distinctly itchy—along with half of the rest of her body—she took the calamine lotion upstairs to her room and happily threw off her clothes. She didn't bathe in the soothing lotion, but by the time she was done dabbing it all over her rashy parts, she almost looked like she had.

Once the liquid was dry, she pulled on loose pajama pants and a camisole and went back downstairs.

Greer was holding Layla, singing softly.

Greer always claimed to be "all about" her career. After watching her with the baby, though, Maddie considered the claim laughable.

Leaving her sister with Layla, she went to the hall closet and dragged out the storage tub containing their Christmas decorations. She set it on the coffee table and worked off the lid. "Don't do all that baby stuff, huh?"

Greer wasn't fazed. "Look, Layla. It's the pink-painted lady."

Maddie spread her arms and twirled once. "Ever fashionable. If Martin could only see me now."

"Who?"

"The guy who stood me up last night."

"I thought his name was Morton."

"Oh. Right." She lifted the baby out of her sister's arms and gestured at the storage bin. "Get to work."

"I will." Greer rubbed her arms. "Do we still have

a window open somewhere? It's finally starting to get a little cool in here."

"I don't know. I'll check in a minute." She grabbed a diaper from the box and laid Layla out on the couch. She peeled her out of the sleeper and changed her. "Then I'm taking this little girl upstairs for a bath."

"In other words, you're using my bathroom."

"It's the only one with a decent tub." When she and her sisters had purchased the house, they'd agreed to be responsible for the renovations of their own bedrooms, but to pool their efforts for the rest of the house. This meant that they could work at their own speed for their own space as they saw fit.

Greer had immediately remodeled her bedroom and en suite. Maddie's was a work in progress. She had an operable shower, but barely. And Ali's was mostly a plan in her mind, which meant she was usually borrowing Maddie's shower.

"True," Greer was saying. "But I'd rather help with Layla's bath than decorate the tree."

"Fine. And when Ali comes home and finds it still undecorated, we'll end up with a tree full of God knows what from the police station." She'd threatened them with Wanted posters, but knowing Ali, the tree would be accessorized by handcuffs and billy clubs.

Greer rolled her eyes and reached into the box. She pulled out a bundle of red and green garland. "Where is our baby sister, anyway?"

A whopping total of thirty minutes had separated their three births. Ali appreciated being called the baby about as much as Maddie appreciated being called by her given name, Maude.

"She probably got called in to work again. You know how her sergeant has been riding her lately."

"Yeah, well, baby sister should have thought about the ramifications before she decided to date then dump her sergeant's son."

"Come on, Greer. That's a little harsh."

"Sorry! But we all know it's never a good idea to be too female in our respective workplaces. It only ends up biting us in the butt."

More so with Ali than either one of them, Maddie thought.

She waited long enough to see that Greer really was putting the garland on the tree, then carried Layla out of the room. She stopped in the laundry room to toss the sleeper into the wash and patrolled the house for open windows before proceeding upstairs to Greer's bathroom.

It was a little chilly, so she turned on the heat lamp before pulling out a clean towel that she spread over the white and black hexagon tiled floor. She settled Layla on the towel while she started the bathwater. Once there were a few inches of warm water and she had soap and towels at the ready, she reached for the baby, who'd managed to get a foot away, simply by virtue of her churning legs. "Not so fast there, speedy." She pulled off the diaper and swung the baby over the edge of the claw-foot tub. Layla squealed, obviously delighted, when her toes hit the water.

"So you like baths." Kneeling next to the tub, Maddie lowered the baby until she was seated, keeping a secure hold of her. "That'll make this nice and easy. I bet your mommy gave you lots and lots of baths." She dunked the washcloth in the water and squeezed it over Layla's shoulders. The baby laughed and Maddie's heart melted. "Oh, sweet pea. I don't know how anyone could leave you." She sluiced more water over her and ran the wet washcloth over her head, turning the soft blond tufts dark. "But we're going to get it all figured out," she murmured. "You're going to have a happy ending. That, I can promise you." She reached for the bar of soap.

The pink lotion she'd spread over her arms was beginning to wash away from the bathwater.

She sighed a little.

She could promise Layla a happy ending.

But she couldn't promise the same thing to Linc.

And she was uncomfortably aware that she was beginning to wish she could.

Chapter Seven

Maddie awkwardly maneuvered the stroller she'd borrowed from one of her most reliable foster moms through the front office door of Swift Oil.

It was Monday morning. There were two inches of snow on the ground outside.

And Maddie had spoken with Judge Stokes's clerk.

A middle-aged woman was sitting behind the modern-looking reception desk and she quickly hopped up when she spotted Maddie and came over to hold open the door for her. "Let me help you."

"Thanks. I think—" she edged the stroller slightly to the left and felt it clear the threshold "—I've got it." She looked over the top of the stroller at Layla, bundled in her fleecy sleeper and the puppy-patterned blanket that had been in the bag of stuff Linc had brought to the house on Saturday. The baby's eyes were bright and blue above the squeaky giraffe she was chewing. The toy had also been in the bag. Along with a rattling ball well-designed for infant hands and a purple, plastic horse.

"Isn't she a sweetheart?" The woman's expression was openly longing as she let the door close and moved around the stroller to admire Layla. "I keep waiting for a grandchild, but so far neither of my sons is cooperating." She finally looked up at Maddie and introduced herself. "I'm Terry. Receptionist and—"

"—gatekeeper."

Maddie's heart jumped in her chest. They both looked over to see Linc. He was standing in one of the hallways that extended from both sides of the reception area.

Terry was much less surprised. "And gatekeeper," she said with a chuckle as she straightened and tugged at the hem of her bulky Christmas sweater. "I was just getting ready to ask this pretty mama what I could do for her."

Maddie flushed. "I'm not Layla's mother. I'm only her care provider," she corrected. "And—"

"—she's here to see me," Linc told Terry. "Layla's my niece."

Terry looked delighted.

Maddie felt dismayed.

"I didn't know your brother had children," Terry said. "Your mother never mentions grandchildren when she comes by the office."

Linc's expression turned sardonic. "You know Jolene. She'd pretend that Jax and I were still in short pants if she could. Otherwise, it's getting harder for her to pretend to still be thirty-nine."

Terry just laughed and swatted her hand at him, as if he were joking. Maddie was fairly certain that he hadn't been. "Go on with the both of you, then. Someone has to work around here."

"Come on back to my office." Linc turned on his heel, disappearing beyond the stylized black wall that bordered Terry's work area. Maddie quickly pushed the stroller forward to follow him.

"Nice meeting you," she told Terry as she passed her.

"You too, honey." The phone on Terry's desk beeped and she reached out to answer it. With her other hand, she waved bye-bye to Layla.

Maddie caught up to Linc only because he was waiting at the point where the hallway turned left in front of a glass wall.

"In here." He stepped aside so she could push the stroller through the door that was propped open.

Why had she ever thought it was such a good idea to tell him about the hearing in person? A phone call would have done just as well. And she could have put off being anywhere near him for another twenty-four hours.

But she was there.

Bing Crosby was softly crooning "Have Yourself a Merry Little Christmas" on the sound system.

She entered the office.

Linc lifted his arm, nearly brushing her shoulder, and she drew in a quick breath.

He merely pushed the door so that it swung shut. It was a glass door. Entirely transparent. It shouldn't feel like he'd just closed out the rest of the world.

But it did.

She slowly exhaled. He was dressed in jeans and heavy work boots, with a dark gray shirt hanging open over a white T-shirt. And though he looked like he'd be more comfortable around an oil rig, he smelled like a guy gracing the cover of *GQ*.

Or how she imagined such a guy would smell.

One part of her wondered how quickly she could get

that seductively woodsy scent out of her head and one part of her wondered how long she could hold on to it.

She watched him move behind a massive wood desk that wasn't the list bit modern. He sat in his chair and leaned back, propping one boot on the corner of his desk as he gestured to the chairs in front of it. "Sit. Otherwise, you look like you're ready to make a run for it."

Great. She felt her face flush and rolled the stroller closer to sit in one of the chairs. She pulled the front of the stroller around so that Layla could still see her, and moved aside the blanket so the baby wouldn't swelter in the warmth of the office.

"Sleeping in your parkas yet?"

She ignored him. Mostly because he wasn't far from the mark and her face was already feeling flushed enough. His and her father's dire predictions about the house getting too cold without the furnace had been pretty accurate. Maddie had kept Layla in bed with her, just to make sure the baby stayed warm enough, and Greer had gone around town borrowing space heaters from their friends. "Judge Stokes scheduled the hearing for tomorrow," she told him baldly. It *was* supposed to be the reason she was there. "Nine a.m. sharp. I was in the area, so I figured I'd save a phone call."

Liar, liar, pants on fire.

She ignored the taunting voice inside her head.

He dropped his boot to the floor and leaned his arms on the papers strewn across the desk. His long fingers closed together. "Sooner than you expected. That's good though?"

"It's not bad," she allowed. She hadn't spoken with him since Saturday. "I should have called to thank you for the calamine."

He lifted a few fingers dismissively. "Doesn't look like you need it so much now."

"Not so much." She made herself lower the hand she'd lifted self-consciously to her cheek. "I don't suppose you've heard from Jax?" She knew it was a long shot and when he shook his head, she wasn't surprised. "And your DNA test? Is it scheduled?"

"I'm heading over to the hospital in Weaver this afternoon about two. Hook's going to meet me there."

"That's good." She leaned over to pick up the giraffe when Layla threw it.

"Want to go with me?"

She nearly dropped the giraffe herself. She handed it back to the baby, trying not to stare at Linc. "I, uh, I—" She broke off and cleared her throat.

"Never mind," Linc said before she could think of what to say. "It was just a thought."

"No, I just—" She broke off when there was a noise behind her, and looked over her shoulder to see Blake Swift pushing through the glass door.

"Linc, what's this bullsh—" Blake abruptly stopped speaking, whether because he realized he had more of an audience than he expected or because of the glacial look that his son was giving him, Maddie couldn't tell.

"Well, well." Blake's expression shifted from annoyance to something else that Maddie couldn't quite put a name to. He strode across the gleaming wood floor to take her hand. "And who is this pretty little thing? I'm sure we've never met." His thumb moved across the back of her hand. "I would certainly have remembered *you*."

Wolfish.

That was what it was.

There could never be any doubt that Blake was Linc's

father. Or any doubt that Linc would be just as handsome in another twenty-some years.

But for all of her opinions about Linc, that expression was one she had never seen on his face. She sincerely hoped that looks were the only thing he'd inherited from his father.

She slid her hand free from Blake's, resisting the urge to wipe it against her jeans as she leaned down to retrieve the giraffe from the floor once again. "Maude Templeton," she said crisply. "And we have met, actually. A long time ago." She'd been eleven.

She looked at Linc. "This afternoon sounds fine." She handed the giraffe to Layla and stood. "I'll leave you to your business."

"Templeton," Blake was murmuring. "The name sounds familiar."

"Maddie," Linc spoke over his father. "You don't have to go."

"I do. I, uh, I have a meeting—"

Blake suddenly snapped his fingers, interrupting her lie. "Maddie. Your mama's Meredith Templeton." His lips curved. "Well, no wonder. You're as pretty as she was. You've got a sister, too, don't you? Twins?"

"Triplets." Like it or not, there were no other sets of triplets in Braden that she was aware of. The locals tended to know who she and her sisters were even if their paths had never specifically crossed, which wasn't the case where Blake was concerned.

She edged around the stroller, keeping her eyes on Linc. "Shall I meet you there?" She felt reluctant to mention exactly *where* they were going in front of his father.

Linc had leaned back in his chair again. "I'll pick you up. No need for us both to drive."

She nodded. "Okay, then." She started forward with the stroller. She couldn't pass Linc's father without saying *something*, but she was darned if she'd tell him it had been nice to see him again. Not when he was the reason her mother had felt forced to stop cleaning for Ernestine all those years ago.

Nevertheless, Maddie managed a polite smile as she steered Layla around him. Because her mother would have her hide if she ever learned Maddie was rude to anyone. Even Blake Swift. "Have a nice afternoon." She pushed the stroller through the still-open door.

Linc thoughtfully watched Maddie's hasty exit.

When she was no longer in sight, he slid his attention to his father.

Blake had thrown himself down in the chair that Maddie had vacated.

"What do you know about Meredith Templeton?" Linc kept his tone mild, but inside he felt anything but.

"She was a sweet piece of—" Blake frowned a little when Linc glared. "Work," he finished. "She used to clean house for Mother, until—" He broke off.

"Until?"

Blake shrugged. "Until she quit."

Linc had never once given any thought to why Maddie's mom had stopped cleaning for Ernestine all those years ago. His grandmother had gone to the same church as Carter and Meredith Templeton. She'd always liked Meredith. Used to say that she had "pluck."

But now, he knew there was a reason.

And that it involved his own father.

"What'd you do? Sleep with her, too?"

Blake huffed, assuming a wounded expression. "No!"

Understanding hit. "She turned you down." Good for Meredith.

Blake's lips twisted. "Don't know why. It's not like she was such a saint. Her reputation—"

"Don't." Linc lifted his hand. "Don't even go there." He couldn't stomach hearing his dad badmouth Maddie's mother. "What'd you barge in here for, anyway?"

"My contact at OKF tells me you're backing out of the deal."

"There was never a deal."

Blake's eyes hardened. "My mother may have left you in charge here, but I still own just as much of an interest in the company as you and Jax do. We've all got a third, sonny boy."

"And without one of the thirds here to side one way or the other, you and I are at a stalemate. Which means no deal." Linc stood. "And the reason why *your* mother left me in charge was because she knew I actually cared about this company. And, because I do care, I've got work to do."

He grabbed his jacket off the coat tree that had belonged to his grandfather. It, along with the desk, were the only things Linc had managed to save when his father had decided it was time to remodel the home office.

Just bringing it into the twenty-first century, Blake had said.

Since Linc had been busy negotiating drilling rights at the time, he'd been happy enough to keep Blake distracted with the remodel…and the pretty architect who'd been the latest to catch Blake's eye.

"That's not work you're thinking about," Blake said now. "It's that pretty little Maddie. You responsible for that baby she's got?"

"What if I am?" He knew what his unsubtle father

was implying and didn't care that his answer would be misconstrued.

Blake just laughed. "Then you're more a chip off this old block than I gave you credit for. Just be careful, boy. You'll marry her, like I married your mama when she got knocked up with you, but she'll end up turning on you the same way Jolene turned on me."

"It's amazing that you still believe you're innocent where Mom is concerned." His mother's infidelities were generally in retaliation for his father's.

Not surprisingly, his father didn't turn a hair. "When Jax gets back, I'll talk him around on the OKF deal," he warned.

"The deal is dead. Period."

"Then I'll find another. Only good thing about Swift Oil is the money it's worth. Money that I can spend a lot better somewhere else besides this bustling metropolis."

"I'm sure you'll try." Blake always did. For as long as he'd lived in Braden, he'd claimed he'd wanted to be elsewhere. Linc pushed his father's shoulder until Blake preceded him out of the office. "And nobody's forcing you to stay here. There's a perfectly good house waiting in Cheyenne that you insisted you had to have. Remember it?" As far as Linc knew, Blake hadn't been there in several years.

"Your mother's there. Drove over yesterday."

"So that's yesterday. What's your excuse been for the last year?" He pulled the door shut. "Don't answer that. I'm not interested in who she is."

"A shame. She has a sister—"

Inured to his father's ways, Linc simply walked away. His dad would either go into his own corner office and try cooking up another headache for Linc to deal with, or not.

He returned to the lobby. "I'm going out to check on Number Five, and then I've got to take care of some business in Weaver," he told Terry. "Anyone calls, I'll get back to them tomorrow."

"Sure thing, Linc." Terry pushed a button on the fancy telephone switchboard. "Merry Christmas," she said cheerfully into her headset. "This is Swift Oil. How can I help you?"

Outside, the ever-present wind was blowing a few snowflakes around and he turned up the collar of his jacket as he walked to his truck. Someone had stuck a circular under his windshield wiper. He pulled it loose, tossing it on his passenger seat as he got inside.

Ordinarily, it took about an hour to drive out to Number Five, which was not the name of a particular well, but the name of an entire oil field. Halfway there, the line of brake lights on the highway warned him it wasn't going to be so quick that day.

He sighed, joining the string of stopped vehicles. He'd wait for a while, but if it took too long, he'd have to turn around and head back to Braden.

He wasn't going to miss the appointment in Weaver no matter what. Not the least because Maddie had agreed to accompany him, though that had been pretty damn surprising.

Almost as surprising as his invitation had been in the first place.

He still didn't know what had gotten into him.

After about ten minutes, the traffic hadn't progressed so much as an inch.

He picked up the flyer from his windshield. There was an advertisement for Christmas Eve church services on one side and a schedule of local holiday events on the other.

The only thing he knew about any of them was that Swift was sponsoring Glitter and Glow that weekend, the same way it had always done. The annual parade had been going on since he'd been a kid. No matter how bad things were between Linc's parents, Ernestine had always made certain that Linc and Jax went to the parade.

He'd have to make sure Layla got to see it, too.

The traffic finally started moving. Linc crumpled the flyer into a ball and tossed it aside.

Maddie paced the length of the living room. It was nearly two o'clock. Linc could be there at any moment.

"Why did I say I'd go?"

She looked over at Layla, who was squirming around on the activity floor mat that Linc had bought. Layla, however, provided no answer. She was more interested in the crinkling, squeaking and vibrating zoo animals that hung from the padded frame arching above the mat from each corner.

Maddie exhaled. She tugged down the sleeves of her sweater. She needed to relax. Get a grip on herself before Linc got there.

She reached the fireplace where the banked fire was doing a good job of keeping the living room toasty, turned and paced back to the staircase. "It's just a trip to the hospital. No big deal." She shoved her sleeves up and made her way toward the fireplace once more.

The oversize flower-patterned purse that she was using as a diaper bag was on the coffee table. She stopped in front of it, checking the provisions she'd packed inside for about the tenth time. It was so full that there was no hope whatsoever of getting the zipper on it closed.

Twelve diapers was probably a little excessive. They wouldn't be gone all day. Just a few hours at the most.

She pulled out half of them and left them on the coffee table, and paced back toward the fireplace. "If we hadn't gone to his office this morning, we wouldn't be in this fix," she told Layla. "I'd have called him about the hearing, and he probably would have mentioned the DNA test." Layla's eyes followed Maddie as she passed her again. "But even if he'd asked us to go, I'd have been able to say no. On the phone. Easy-peasy." She stopped in front of the improvised diaper bag. Shoved three of the ones she'd just taken out back inside. "Maybe another bottle of formula," she said. "Just in case there's a delay."

Layla managed to bat the vibrating monkey with her waving hands and then let out a toothless smile and a laugh.

"Right." Maddie exhaled again and went into the kitchen. She'd unpacked the case of ready-to-use formula and stacked the bottles in one of the doorless wall cabinets. She pulled one down, then muttered an oath when it caused an avalanche of the others. She tried catching them before they all rolled right out of the cabinet, but managed to save only a few. "Swift, Maddie." She crouched down to corral the escapees. One had rolled all the way to the refrigerator and she crawled after it.

"Still not locking your door, I see."

She jerked back, knocking her head against the frame of a base cabinet. "*Must* you keep sneaking up on me?" She rubbed the back of her stinging head and glared at Linc. And immediately wished that he didn't look so darned good when she was always feeling so darned…not.

"Lock your doors like you should." He extended his hand.

He meant to help her up. She knew that. Instead of taking his hand, she plunked the bottle of formula into his palm and pushed to her feet all by herself. She still had a rashy patch on her right forearm and she yanked her sleeves back down where they belonged. "Stop going through doors whether they're locked or not."

His lips twitched. It was the closest thing to an actual smile that she'd seen on his face in more than a decade.

And darned if her heart didn't go all aflutter.

Far more annoyed with herself than him, she plucked the formula out of his hand and went back into the living room where she tucked the bottle into the already-stuffed purse, alongside the one she'd already prepped with the nipple and cap. "We're ready to go. I just need to buckle her into her carrier."

"No need."

Something inside her nosedived. "Oh." She didn't look at him as she went to the fireplace and picked up the poker. "You didn't need to come by. You could have just called." She moved the screen a few inches so she could jab the burning wood. A flurry of sparks exploded, dancing up the flue.

"To notify you that I had a car seat installed in the truck?"

She looked over her shoulder at him. She'd thought he was canceling. "What?"

He crossed to her and took the poker out of her hand. "I feel better around you when you're not armed." He hung it back on the hook and replaced the fireplace screen. "You need a permanent screen."

"Um." She curled her fingers against her palm and tried not to sound as bemused as she was. "Why?"

He lifted the three-panel screen. "Hardly baby-proof. I'll make sure you get one." He set the screen back in place.

"That's not—" She broke off at the look he gave her. She'd been about to say *necessary*. But what was the point? He was going to do what he wanted to do no matter what she said. And she didn't have the heart to remind him again how small the chances were of Layla staying for any length of time with either one of them. "We should get moving," she said instead. She pulled on her coat. "I've heard the highway's been a mess today with the ice." She picked up the baby and the bulging purse.

"It has. Almost didn't make it out to Number Five at all." He took the purse from her, his gaze lingering on the contents. "You packing for the night?"

"No. So don't go getting any ideas that I've changed my mind about staying with you." She felt more flushed than ever. "I mean staying at your house."

He looked amused as he pulled open the door for her, gesturing for her to precede him. "Take notes. I'm turning the lock, such as it is." He flipped the knob lock with exaggerated care. "I assume you do have a key?"

"I have a key."

He pulled the door closed, then took her elbow. "Watch the steps."

She had been going up and down the front steps of the house ever since she and her sisters purchased it. Two years of step navigating. Summers and winters and everything in between. But she didn't pull her elbow away.

When they reached his truck, he opened the back door, displaying the expensive-looking car seat. She couldn't even imagine where he got such a fancy one around Braden at all, much less on such short notice. She fit Layla into the seat and fastened the harness. Then she handed her the giraffe and stepped back down to the ground.

"You're not sitting back there with her this time?"

Great. "I, uh, I tend to get carsick in the back seat on long rides." She'd never been carsick in her entire life.

He shut the door for her without responding and crossed around the front to get behind the wheel.

She'd already buckled herself in and tucked her oddly nervous hands between her knees. "I've never known why the Number Five field has that name," she said once he pulled away from the house. "I mean, there aren't fields named Numbers One through Four."

He gave her a sideways look. "You've never been out to the oil field?"

She shook her head. "Should I have?"

"Schools send students out there on field trips at least once a year these days."

Despite herself, she chuckled. "I haven't been a schoolkid for quite some time now."

"I noticed."

A quiver slid down her spine. She blamed it on the truck tires rumbling over a rough spot in the road. "So why is it named Number Five?"

"That's how many times my grandfather proposed to my grandmother before she accepted."

"You're joking."

He shrugged. "Look it up."

"I will. So you better not be pulling my leg."

His lips twitched. "What're you going to do if I am? Report me to the police?"

"Now I know you're joking."

"Suit yourself. But if you'd ever been out there, you'd see there's a plaque about it and everything."

"No man in his right mind would propose *five* times. He'd give up!"

Linc's hazel gaze slid over her. "Maybe Gus considered Ernestine worth the effort."

For some stupid reason, she felt that quiver again and now she had no rough road to blame it on.

She gave him a cross look. "Keep your eyes on the road. The last thing we need is to get in an accident."

He smiled outright.

Maddie swallowed hard and looked out the window. *It's just a trip to the hospital. No big deal.*

Yeah. Right.

Chapter Eight

"All right." Justin Clay slid the last cheek swab into a vial, capped it and affixed a label preprinted with Linc's information over it. "My lab's pretty backed up right now, but we should have the results in a week." He glanced at Tom Hook. "You'll want a copy, I assume?"

The older man nodded. "I'd appreciate it." Since his part was done, he shook Linc's hand and left.

Justin looked at Linc. "You realize we're going to need something to compare your results against, right? Otherwise, it's simply an interesting genetic study."

Maddie held her breath. She hadn't specifically addressed the issue with Linc, but when he glanced at her, she knew it didn't matter.

"I know," he said. "I want it ready, though, when we *can* compare it against Layla's. I don't want any time wasted. At least on the things I can control."

"Good enough. DNA typing is all a puzzle of percentages. So it would help if we had more profiles than just you and Layla to compare—Jax, her mother, other possible fathers—but I guess if they were available, you wouldn't be here like this." Justin spun around on his metal stool and placed the vials on a tray on the metal table behind him. Then he turned to face Linc again as he pulled off his sterile gloves. "I've been meaning to call your office," he said. "Set up a meeting to talk about some equipment we're hoping to upgrade."

Justin not only ran the hospital lab, he was also Maddie's cousin, a fact that had only been discovered after her grandmother had moved to Wyoming. "I thought you just finished expanding the lab," she said. Thanks in no small part to Vivian's significant financial contribution.

"We did." He gestured with one arm and grinned. "Now we want to fill it with some more cool stuff. I know Swift Oil has been a big supporter of the hospital in the past."

"I'm sure we can work something out," Linc assured him. "Thanks for helping me with the test. I didn't expect personal attention from the lab director himself."

"Glad to help." Justin wiggled Layla's foot. "Seems like yesterday when Gracie was this little. Now, she's already a year old and running circles around Tabby and me."

"They do grow fast," Maddie agreed. "Are you two going to Vivian's Christmas party?"

Justin smiled ruefully. "Don't think there is any way of getting out of it since my wife already has her dress. Although, if Gloria has her way and actually manages to get Squire to go, there are sure to be some entertaining fireworks."

Maddie laughed. Squire was Justin's grandfather.

To say there was no love lost between him and Vivian was an understatement. The two seniors had even run against each other earlier that year for a seat on the Weaver Town Council.

Vivian had lost, but not by much. And considering she was a relative newcomer to the area—whereas Squire Clay had been ranching there since the dawn of time—that was a feat in itself.

"I really can't see your grandfather crossing my grandmother's doorstep no matter how persuasive Squire's wife can be," she said. "But that would probably be entertaining."

Justin glanced at the clock on the wall then back at Linc. "I don't mean to swab and run, but I've got another appointment. I'll have one of my techs show you the way out." The lab didn't have a complicated layout, but it was secured behind locked doors.

"Thanks." Linc shook his hand, and then Justin hurried off, his white coat flapping around his long legs. A moment later, one of Justin's staff escorted them out of the area.

Maddie chewed the inside of her cheek as the security door swung closed with a soft click, leaving them in an antiseptically austere tiled hallway. Their footsteps echoed as they headed down it toward the elevator. "I know what you're thinking." She had to hurry a little to keep up with Linc's long-legged stride.

"That your grandmother's Christmas party sounds like the hot ticket in town?"

"No. Well," she allowed quickly, "I suppose it sounds like it."

"At least your family does something together, even if it is full of fireworks." Along with his jacket and Maddie's coat, he was also still carrying the overstuffed flowered purse. It ought to have looked silly hanging off his broad shoulder.

Instead, Maddie was well aware of the number of appreciative female glances he'd garnered when they'd entered the hospital. She could only imagine how much more appreciative they'd have been had he also been carrying the baby.

There was just something about a man tending a baby.

About *him* tending a baby.

She swallowed down the disturbing notion. "I meant about Layla also needing a DNA test."

They'd reached the elevator and Linc's shoulder brushed against hers when he reached out to press the call button. The doors immediately slid open. "I can manage to figure out a few things on my own." His voice was dry.

"Then you understand why I couldn't just have Layla's test done today, too?"

He put one hand on the doors to make sure they stayed open. "Yes. You going to get on the elevator? Or do you want to just stand here in the hall for a while?"

She carried Layla onto the empty elevator, moving to the rear corner. When he took the opposite corner, she wondered if it was simply habit, or if he too felt the need to keep some space between them. "I wasn't trying to keep you in the dark about it."

"I know."

"It's a matter of privacy," she added doggedly, because she wanted him to be really clear on the matter. "Even though she's an infant, Layla has rights we have to protect—"

"I *get* it, Maddie."

She pressed her lips together.

They both focused on the elevator display. The car seemed to take forever moving from one floor to the next, and there were only three. She didn't even realize that she'd been holding her breath, until the doors slid open again and she hurried through them.

The main floor of the hospital was considerably busier than the third floor had been. They'd barely gotten out of the elevator before people were quickly stepping into it.

She didn't pay them any attention until one of them said her name. "Maddie?"

She glanced back at the man. She'd only met him once, when he'd been with her boss. But she still recognized him. "Mar—Morton." She was painfully aware that Linc had stopped to look, too. "What a surprise."

Morton smiled genially, as if he hadn't just stood her up a few days earlier. "I'm the one who works here. I think that makes your presence more a surprise than mine." His eyes were frankly curious as he took in Layla and Linc. "I was sorry that things didn't work out last Friday. We can try again this week, if you're available."

She just stared at him, not sure at all how to respond. He was about Linc's age, had half the hair, and none of the washboard abs. Not that she'd ever seen Morton without his shirt. She hadn't needed to. But when she'd met him the one time with her boss, he'd seemed nice enough.

Until he'd left her sitting for an hour at the restaurant where they'd agreed to meet before she'd finally given up on him and left.

"I...don't think so," she told him.

Linc's hand suddenly closed over Maddie's shoulder and she nearly jumped out of her skin. "Aren't you going to introduce us?"

She hesitated.

That was all Linc needed, evidently, and she watched with some horrified bemusement when he extended his other hand toward Martin. *Morton!*

"Lincoln Swift," he said.

Morton's expression grew even more curious as he shook Linc's hand. "Morton Meadows."

"So, Morton. How do you know our Maddie?"

Maddie shuffled her feet, but Linc's hand didn't drop away from her shoulder. "He's a friend of my boss," she said abruptly. It was bad enough to have been stood up. She didn't particularly want Linc knowing about it, too.

"Well, a friend of yours, too," Morton said with a chuckle.

She felt her jaw loosen a little. "Uh, sure. Whatev—"

Mercifully, Layla decided to take center stage at that moment, opening her mouth and letting out a loud wail.

Maddie jiggled the baby, who'd been an angel up to that point. "She's sleepy and probably hungry by now." She pulled the pacifier out of the purse Linc was holding and looked up at him. The baby turned her face away from the pacifier and wailed louder. "We should—"

"Go," he finished. "Good idea." He gave Morton a dismissive smile that Maddie couldn't help but enjoy as they turned and headed toward the hospital exit again. Only when they reached it did Linc's hand finally move away from her shoulder.

He held up her coat. "You'll want this. It's started snowing again."

She looked through the glass entrance. Sure enough, the snow was falling again. She knew there was no point in trying to hand Layla to him, particularly with the way she was crying, which meant Maddie had to suffer through him helping her on with her coat while she shifted the fussing baby from one arm to the other.

But when he started to button her in, she couldn't take anymore and she quickly stepped away. "I'm good. Thanks." She tried offering the pacifier to Layla again, but the baby still wanted nothing to do with it.

"Hold on." Linc gestured at the arrangement of chairs near the doors. He set the purse on one of them, pulled out the premixed bottle and uncapped it.

Maddie exchanged the pacifier for the bottle, and Layla went to town on it, her cries immediately ceasing. Maddie swirled the puppy blanket up and around the baby. "Okay," she said, feeling a little breathless. "We're good now."

"We can sit here if you want."

She already felt like they'd been drawing more than enough attention. "She'll be fine finishing in the truck."

He looped the long strap of the flowery purse over his shoulder again and they headed out.

The snow danced around them, but Maddie didn't mind. She felt overheated to her bones, courtesy of the hand that he lightly pressed against the small of her back as they walked through the parking lot.

When they reached the truck, she passed him Layla's bottle long enough to get the baby latched into her seat, then hurriedly climbed up beside her again.

"Not worried about getting carsick?"

Their fingers brushed when she quickly took the bottle back from him and offered it once more to Layla. "She can't hold the bottle by herself yet."

That was true, at least.

He reached in and set the purse near her feet. Then

he straightened and his eyes met hers, probably not even intentionally.

But she still felt something in her chest squeeze.

His eyebrows drew together. "What?"

She shook her head and made herself push some words out through her tightening throat. "You have a snowflake on your nose." And on his hair. On his shoulders. Like nature had decided to sprinkle him with glistening sugar.

He brushed his hand over his perfect nose and closed the truck door.

She let out a shaky breath and managed to somehow fasten her own seatbelt one-handed since Layla was adamantly opposed to having the bottle nipple move even an inch away from her.

Then Linc was getting in behind the wheel, and starting up the truck. He flipped on the wipers and they brushed easily through the snow accumulating on the windshield. Maddie imagined she could feel his gaze on her through the rearview mirror, but kept her own strictly on the baby. He steered the truck out of the hospital parking lot and within minutes, they were leaving the town behind.

The only sounds were the engine, the thrum of tires on the snowy highway and the sweet, soft noises Layla made as she guzzled.

Maddie leaned her head against her seat and unfastened her coat. She started to relax.

"So what's the story with Meadows?"

So much for relaxing.

She focused on Layla. "There's no story."

"Two of you sleep together or something?"

She looked up, gaping at him in the rearview mirror. "No!"

"Yeah. Figured. No chemistry between the two of you at all."

She huffed. "Then why even say such a thing!"

"Because it's pretty entertaining seeing the way you react."

She rolled her eyes. If her cheeks were as red as they felt, she would look in need of calamine lotion again. "You're annoying."

He actually chuckled.

She would have been even more annoyed at that, if she weren't flabbergasted to hear him laugh.

"He stood me up for dinner," she admitted severely. "No meal together, much less anything else."

"So he's an idiot. What about Jax?"

The baby bottle almost slid out of her hand. She quickly adjusted it before Layla could get riled up. "What about him?"

"Sleep with him?"

She opened her mouth. Closed it again. Shook her head. "This is not a conversation we are having," she muttered as much for her own benefit as his.

"So you did."

"No, I did not sleep with Jax!"

"Ever?"

She kicked the back of his seat. She'd rather have kicked him, but since she was not a violent person, it had to do. "I was seventeen when you told me I needed to stay far, *far* away from Jax."

"Which isn't an answer."

She kicked his seat again. "I wasn't sleeping with him at seventeen! Or eighteen, or any other time. And none of it's your business anyway! Not Martin or Jax or—"

"Who's Martin?"

"Morton!" She thumped her head against her seat-back. "Just…just be quiet. My sex life—" *or lack of it*, she amended quietly to herself "—is none of your business. I'm not asking *you* about the women you've slept with." Just the thought of them was enough to make her feel jealous, and she hated that fact.

"Been a while, has it?"

She closed her eyes and threw her free arm over her face for good measure. She'd choke before she told him just how long a while. The last date she'd had was almost a year ago. As for sex, that was even longer ago. "Whatever this game is, I'm not playing."

He chuckled again. "You're pretty cute when you're pissed off."

"I must be cute around you all the time, then," she muttered.

"So when is your grandmother's party supposed to be?"

"Night before Christmas Eve." She dropped her arm and watched his forehead in the rearview mirror. "And why are you being so chatty, anyway?"

"It's better than thinking about those cheek swabs or what that judge of yours is going to say tomorrow morning."

He couldn't have said anything more effective.

All of her annoyance drizzled out of her.

Layla hadn't quite finished the bottle, but her eyes were closed, so Maddie fit the cap back on the bottle and dropped it inside the purse. "Linc, even if the judge doesn't rule in your favor tomorrow morning, it doesn't mean that Layla's going to disappear somewhere terrible. I promise you, she would be with very qualified caregivers. I would see to it personally."

"That doesn't make this any better."

She leaned forward as far as her seatbelt allowed, and touched her fingers to his shoulder. "I know. But you're doing everything right here. If you're her uncle—"

"What if I'm not?"

She hesitated. "You've been adamant that you are." She hadn't considered that he'd allowed any room for doubt, no matter what her opinions might have been. "And you know, Jax will come back. Like you said. He always comes back. He's just off somewhere skiing or... or something. Chances are, he'll show up and explain all of this. Who Layla's mother is. Why she would have left Layla the way she did. And he'll do what's right."

"If he even recognizes what's right," Linc murmured. "He's with Dana. My ex-wife."

Maddie blinked. She wasn't sure if her "Oh," escaped her lips or if it was just sounding inside her head. "I'm sorry," she finally managed. She didn't know what else to say.

"Me, too." The tires hummed in the silence. "For him. He should have learned his lesson where she's concerned by now." He was silent for another moment. "He's too much like our parents. Maybe he never will learn."

She sincerely hoped he would learn. His mom and dad had never been any sort of parents. She'd recognized that even as a kid. It had been Ernestine who'd provided her grandsons with love and attention and boundaries. Was it going to be left to Linc to do the same with Layla? "If he's with your, uh, with Dana, then do you know how to reach them?"

"I know who he's with. Doesn't mean that I know where."

She chewed the inside of her lip. "You don't think that Dana is Layla's—"

"No." Linc's voice was flat.

She let it drop even though her head was about to explode with unasked questions. "Right now, let's just take it one step at a time. The first step is the hearing tomorrow morning."

He made a sound. Of agreement, she supposed.

She looked over at Layla. The baby's sleeping face was angelic, and she lightly grazed her fingertip over her soft, soft hair.

Then she had to close her eyes, because they were suddenly burning with tears.

The next morning, Maddie beat Linc to the courthouse.

In fact, she and Layla seemed to beat everyone.

When Maddie pushed the stroller through Judge Stokes' courtroom door, the room was empty.

She didn't worry, though. She knew she was a few minutes early. But it had just been easier to come to the courthouse than keep huddling around the space heaters and the fireplace at home, because the temperature had dropped another ten degrees since the day before.

There were three rows of wooden bench seats on either side of the center aisle behind the bar, and she maneuvered the stroller into the front row.

She unwrapped the blanket tucked around Layla and smiled into her face, squeezing the squeaking giraffe until the baby chortled and grabbed the giraffe for herself. Layla squeezed it, too, and jumped when it squeaked, then laughed all over again.

Maddie cupped her hand tenderly over the baby's head. "Sweet girl."

"What the *hell* are you doing here, Templeton?"

Maddie jumped, dropping her hand. She looked

around to see Raymond Marx standing in the doorway of the courtroom. To say her forty-year-old boss looked displeased was putting it mildly. His bald head was red, his wrinkled tie was more askew than usual, and he was sweating. As if he'd run all the way to the courtroom from their office down the street.

He approached her and jabbed a finger in the air. "I warned you. No cases for two weeks."

"Ray—"

"Don't *Ray* me. You do this all the time, and I told you it had to stop. You're going to burn out and quit, and I'm going to lose my best worker." He reached her row and put his hands over the stroller handle.

Panic shot through her and she grabbed the side of the stroller. She wasn't sure what she could do if he decided to take Layla from her, but she knew she couldn't let it happen.

"Best worker or not, you had no right approaching the judge the way you did. This is an agency matter and you know it."

She opened her mouth to defend herself, but he raised his palm, silencing her. "You're off this case as of right now."

"But—"

"And while I decide what to do with you, instead of vacationing for the next two weeks, consider yourself suspended instead. Without pay. Maybe then you'll take me seriously."

She shoved off the bench. "That is *not* fair."

"What's not fair is you thinking you don't have to follow the rules."

"I have followed the rules," she said hotly. "Every single one. Except the vacation guideline. Guideline! You forced my vacation, and you know it. And while *on vacation*, I assessed Layla's situation when I became aware of it. I saw to the safety of this child, and I reported it!"

"To the court," he said through his teeth. "What about to your boss?"

"Good morning, Ray." Judge Horvald Stokes ambled into the courtroom from the door behind the bench, carrying his coffee and a doughnut. He was at least twenty years older than Ray, and had all of the hair that Ray did not. It was just bright white. As was his beard. Which tended to make Judge Stokes look a little like Santa Claus, particularly when he wore a red sweater, as he was now. "You're sounding in rare form this morning." He lifted his doughnut in cheer. "Morning, Miss Maddie."

She swallowed, reminding herself that what she had done was nothing illegal, but just outside of protocol where her stickler of a boss was concerned. "Good morning, Your Honor."

The judge approached to peer over the stroller at Layla. "Aren't you the cute one?" Then he headed back to the ramp that led up to his bench. He set down his coffee and swallowed half of his doughnut. "Ray, your knickers tighter than usual this morning for some reason?"

"No, Your Honor."

"So you look like you're gonna have a stroke every morning?"

Ray gave her a fulminating look, as if this were all her fault. Which she supposed it was. "No, Your Honor," he said grimly. "Just an internal matter that's causing me some…concern."

The judge smiled. "Well. I'm not one to get into

your internal matters. So what say you settle it outside of my courtroom?"

"With pleasure." Ray started to pull the stroller away from Maddie.

She held fast. "Don't do this, Ray. You can suspend me if you want. Fire me for that matter. But this child is in *my* protective custody right now. Not the department's."

"If it weren't for the department—"

"I'd have still called Maddie."

They both turned to see Linc entering. His intense eyes lingered on her face as he approached. Tom Hook was with him. "What's going on here?"

"Internal matters," Judge Stokes said dryly. He swallowed down the other half of his doughnut and pulled on his black robe, though he didn't bother with zipping it up. "Morning, Tom. Good to see you. Been a while." The side door swung open, and the court reporter came in, carrying his steno writer, followed by the clerk and the court officer. As usual, the judge greeted them all by name. Typically, Judge Stokes liked to keep everyone comfortable.

Until he didn't. Then he'd zip up his robe, and it would be all business. Period.

Maddie was following the proceedings with one ear. The rest of her was focused on Linc, her boss and Layla. The baby's face was scrunching up as if she sensed the tension around her and Maddie made herself relax. She sat down on the long wooden seat and squeezed the giraffe a few times. "Everything's fine, sweet pea."

"This isn't going to be the last of it," Ray warned her. But even he didn't have the nerve to interrupt when the court was called into session.

Tom and Linc sat at the table in front of her, Ray at the other.

She should have called Archer to come and represent her. She just honestly hadn't thought she'd need him.

The court clerk read off the details of the hearing, then handed Judge Stokes a sheaf of papers.

"Thank you, Sue." The judge folded his arms in front of him atop the papers he set on his desk. He looked at them all in turn. "So," he said. "We've got what appears to be an abandoned infant. That still the case?" He glanced up with an arched brow. Receiving no correction, he continued. "All right. That leaves us with the question of what to do about that."

Ray popped out of his seat like an overwound jack-in-the-box toy. "Your Honor, my department is fully prepared to handle the matter and I apologize that you were called in prematurely—"

The judge lifted his palm, silencing Ray the same way that Ray had silenced Maddie. "Let's just focus on the child for the moment. Aside from the note you referenced in the filing, is there anyone in this room who can tell me for certain who she is?"

Tom Hook stood.

Judge Stokes looked at him. "For *certain*, Tom?"

"No, Your Honor. But my client is working to that end."

"Good for your client." The judge focused on Linc. "What is it that you hope to prove, Mr. Swift?"

Linc stood. He was wearing a black suit and was easily the most formally dressed one there. And Maddie could see just how tight his broad shoulders were. "That Layla is my niece. My brother's child. Though I don't believe he was aware of that fact."

"And your brother?" The judge glanced through the papers. "Jaxon Swift. Why isn't he here today?"

"Mr. Swift's brother is out of town," Tom interjected. "My client is making every effort to reach him. I can't emphasize enough that he is very certain his brother is unaware that any of this has occurred."

The judge looked from Linc's table to Ray's, then back again. "I knew your grandmother, Mr. Swift," he said suddenly. "A good woman."

"Yes," Linc agreed quietly. "She was."

"Mmm." The judge flipped through the papers again. "This is a problem. Suppositions aside, we have an unknown mother. Unknown father. Going to involve a heck of an investigation."

Maddie swallowed. She reached into the stroller and plucked Layla out of it, holding her close. Not because Layla needed it.

But because she did.

Particularly when the judge sat back and suddenly zipped his robe.

Chapter Nine

The judge looked at his clerk. "You awake there, Sue?"

Sue gave him a look.

"Just checking." Judge Stokes looked out at them again. "All right then. I want a thorough investigation where Layla's parents are concerned. To that end, I'm ordering genetic testing of Layla." His expression was solemn. "Let's get it ruled out that someone somewhere else isn't frantically searching for their child. And—" he eyed Linc "—I'll allow the comparison to the results you're submitting. If anything comes of that, then we'll be meeting here again sooner rather than later."

"Thank you, Your Honor," Tom said.

The judge nodded briefly. He looked toward Ray. "Meanwhile, baby Layla will require suitable shelter care until a custodian—whether Mr. Swift or another party—is named."

Maddie sucked in a quick breath and stood. "I'm suitable."

Even across the room she could hear her boss groan. "Maddie Templeton is presently on suspension."

The judge sighed a little. "That internal matter, I suppose."

"Yes."

"If my suspension is an issue, then I'll quit." Her voice was husky but it was still clear.

Linc turned around and looked at her.

She kept her eyes on the judge. "I'm a qualified foster-care provider, Judge." A fact that he knew perfectly well. "Whether I'm employed by the department or not."

The judge tapped his thumbs together a few times. "What's the basis for Miss Maddie's suspension, Ray? She's always seemed very capable to me."

"Ignoring departmental rules."

"With regard to what?"

"Vacation," Maddie inserted quickly.

The judge looked pained. "Is that true, Ray?"

"Well, yes."

"Not abuse of power. Not dereliction of duties. Not even using the office copier for her own personal use. Which is something we have all done anyway."

"No." Ray straightened his wrinkled tie. "If anything, Maddie is too far the opposite. She's determined that every family finds a happy ending and you know how impossible that is. She takes cases to the extreme."

"Sort of like taking vacation rules to the extreme?" The judge's voice turned dry.

"She took on a case when she shouldn't have," Ray maintained doggedly.

"Your Honor," Tom interrupted. "Considering my client's desire to care for this child he believes to be his niece, he could have chosen not to notify anyone at all and none of us would be the wiser. But knowing of her expertise, he chose to reach out to Miss Templeton for assistance."

The judge pursed his lips as he looked at Linc, who'd faced forward once again. "Why Maddie?" He lifted his hand. "Cool your jets, Tom. Let your client answer. I just want to know."

"She's an old friend," Linc said evenly.

"So you didn't contact her in an official capacity."

"No." He waited a beat. "She very quickly advised me of her legal obligations, though."

The judge smiled slightly. "I'll bet she did." He tapped his thumbs together a few more times. "You married, Mr. Swift?"

"Not anymore."

"Too bad. Kids?"

"No."

"Dogs? Cats?" The judge lifted his hand. "Don't answer that." He looked toward Ray. "I can't tell you what to do about your sacred vacation rule, Ray. But seems to me that you're wound up over a whole lot of nothing." Then he looked at Maddie. "You're willing to provide a safe and stable environment for baby Layla? See to all of her needs, physically and otherwise?"

"Yes, Your Honor."

He nodded once. "Good enough. Look sharp, everyone," he said. "I'm ordering that Layla temporarily remain in the care of Maddie Templeton. And I want an update on the investigation and the baby's care in one week's time when I will reassess the matter. Got that, Sue?"

"Got it, Judge."

He slammed his gavel once. "Adjourned."

Then he stood up, unzipped his black judge's robe and disappeared through the back door to his chambers.

"Congratulations." Tom shook Linc's hand. "Stay of execution, as it were."

"For a week." Linc looked at Maddie where she was sitting on the bench behind them, hugging Layla to her. Maddie was pale. His chest felt tight. "Only because of her," he said gruffly.

Tom shrugged. "It's still a win in your column for today. Meanwhile, my advice is to find your brother before the authorities do. Get him back here. And stay in touch with me."

Linc nodded. "Thanks, Tom." He shook the lawyer's hand. "I will."

The lawyer moved away. He leaned over, murmuring something to Maddie on his way out of the courtroom.

Maddie smiled a little, then sobered when her eyes met Linc's.

"You wouldn't really quit your job over this," he said.

She rubbed her cheek against Layla's blond hair. "Fortunately, we don't have to find out." She stood.

The rumpled guy who was obviously her boss stopped next to them. "Maybe suspension is a bit much."

She lifted an eyebrow. "You think?"

"Don't push it, Templeton." He studied the baby in her arms. Layla had tucked her thumb in her mouth and was looking drowsy and very comfortable nestled against Maddie's chest. "Prosecutor's going to want the note."

Maddie looked quickly at Linc. "You still have it, right?"

He reached in his lapel pocket and withdrew the

small piece of paper. "I kept a copy of it for myself." His lips twisted slightly. "Used the office copier."

Maddie bit her lip, looking down at her toes.

Ray took the note and unfolded it. He shook his head. "I hope for everyone's sake this doesn't get messier before it gets better." He patted the baby's back gently. "See you here next week." Then he strode away, too.

Maddie's chocolate gaze lifted to Linc's once more. "My house is freezing," she said baldly. "And that swing you got for her won't fit in my car. You'll have to pick it up."

He squelched the leaping sensation inside him. "You've come to your senses."

"No. I'm pretty sure I've lost them." She started to lower Layla into the stroller but the baby squawked out a protest. "My parents' house is perfectly well-heated, too." She dropped her too-full flowered purse into the stroller and grabbed the handle with her free hand, steering it clear of the bench seat. "And my mother *loves* babies."

He covered her hand with his and she went still. "Then why?"

"Because it's the right thing to do."

"For Layla."

Her gaze slid away. Her voice went husky. "And for you."

Then she shifted, pulling away from him. She pushed the stroller toward the courtroom doors, but stopped just shy of them. She looked back at him where he still stood, feeling rooted to the ground. "I'll need a key to your house." She was back to her usual briskness.

"I'll get you whatever you need."

Something came and went in her eyes. "Let's just start with the key."

Then she turned and pushed the stroller through the courtroom door.

Linc slowly sank back down onto the chair. He wasn't used to feeling like the stuffing had been pulled right out of him. He stared at the courtroom around him. It had emptied entirely after the judge exited.

She'd been willing to quit her job.

He rubbed his hand down his face but he couldn't rub away the shock he'd felt when she'd said it to the judge. Or the way her expression has been so certain.

The side door opened and Sue, the court clerk, entered. She stopped in surprise when she spotted him. "Mr. Swift. I'm sorry. I didn't realize you were still here. Was there something else you needed?"

He knew she was married to one of his engineers and wondered how often she had to clerk for some case involving a Swift Oil employee. "No, I was just thinking if these courtroom walls could talk."

"They'd know better than to try." She seemed cheerful enough as she set a stack of files on her desk, clearly getting ready for the next case.

He pushed to his feet. "I guess I'll be seeing you next week."

She smiled. "Jerry's always telling me what a decent man you are, Mr. Swift. I wish you good luck with all of this."

"Thanks, Sue."

"Merry Christmas."

He smiled faintly. For the first time in a long time, he actually felt a little anticipation where the holiday was concerned. "Merry Christmas to you, too."

A loud thump vibrated through the walls, making Maddie jump nervously.

She looked at Layla, lying on the changing table inside the nursery at Linc's home. "Sounds like Uncle Linc is back," she said. Rather than leave the nursery to go and see, though, she finished fastening Layla's diaper and then tucked her into one of the stretchy knit sleepers that Ali had produced when she'd come home after her shift to find Maddie packing her suitcase. "He's going to think you're pretty as a picture in your new clothes."

Layla kicked her legs enthusiastically. Her eyes danced as she looked up at Maddie.

The adoration in the baby's eyes was almost too much to bear.

She picked up the baby, cuddling her close. Maddie had given Layla her bath and she smelled like everything that could possibly be right in this world. "Of course," she whispered, "even without all your new things you're pretty as a picture."

"It's a picture all right," Linc said, walking into the nursery. He was still wearing the suit from that morning, but the tie was gone and the top two buttons of his white shirt were undone. "Where do you want this?"

She quickly looked from the strong column of his throat to the infant swing he was carrying. "That's a good question." She glanced around the nursery. It had been perfectly spacious the first time she'd seen it. Now there were boxes of baby items everywhere. While she'd been packing clothes to last her for the coming week, she felt certain he'd sent someone to Shop-World in Weaver to buy out the entire baby department. "Wherever you can find room."

He smiled slightly. "It is a little crowded in here now."

He had enough gear to outfit half a dozen nurseries.

And they didn't even know what would happen with Layla once the next week passed.

"A little," she agreed. With her foot, she nudged a tricycle into the corner. It would be two years before Layla would be ready for the thing. "Here." Moving the trike had freed up a few spare feet of floor space.

He deposited the swing in the spot and glanced through the doorway to the adjoining room. "You get yourself settled all right?"

"Yes. You didn't have to send over Terry with keys this afternoon, though. We could have just waited until this evening to come here."

"She had some other errands to take care of for me, so she was already out and about." He picked up one of the sleepers from Ali that Maddie had yet to put away in the chest of drawers. "Fitting for the season," he drawled. The sleeper was fashioned like something Santa's elves would wear. The one that Layla currently had on was dark blue and covered in white snowflakes. "Looks like someone else has been doing some shopping, too."

"Blame Ali. I haven't had time to take care of anything except the necessities, much less go shopping. It's a good thing you bought so many diapers the other day. We're going through them like nobody's business." Maddie settled Layla into the seat of the swing. It was surprising how heavy a fifteen-pound baby could be. "The only things we're still missing are extra bottles and nipples. Pretty much the most basic of basic." She snapped the safety harness together and turned on the swing. Fortunately, it also ran on batteries, because there was no way the power cord could have reached its spot in virtually the center of the nursery.

The unicorns, no longer looking scrunched up from

being packaged in a box, began slowly revolving above Layla's head as the seat of the swing started swaying.

Linc was watching Layla so intently that Maddie felt a stab somewhere in the vicinity of her heart. "Listen." She snatched up the damp bath towels from the rocker where she'd dumped them. "I left a bit of a mess in the bathroom. If you wouldn't mind sitting with her for a few, I'll just get it cleaned up." There was no earthly reason why she couldn't have nipped into the adjoining bathroom for a few minutes to take care of tidying up when Layla was so securely contained in the swing, but she didn't figure he needed to know that. "Here." She patted the upholstered chair in invitation, and carried the towels out of the room.

She didn't wait to see what he would do. Because she knew if she did, he wouldn't do anything.

The bathroom was a Jack and Jill, opening to both the nursery and Maddie's bedroom. She went through the door and turned on the water, making as much noise as she could to prove how necessary her task was. She pushed the door to the nursery partially closed and used one of the towels to mop up the water that she and Layla had splashed onto the cream-colored tile. While she was crawling around on the floor, she peeked around the door to see if any progress had been made in the nursery.

Linc was sitting on the rocker. He'd discovered the video baby monitor box that she'd yet to unpack. His eyes, however, were trained on the bathroom doorway.

She flushed and backed out of view.

"I still see you," he said.

She sat up on her knees and caught her reflection in the mirror over the sink. "Still see me what?" she asked innocently. But her cheeks were red. She climbed to her feet and spread the wet towels over the side of the tub and the separate glass shower enclosure. She figured with a little practice, she'd be able to bathe Layla without creating a swamp on the floor, but for now, she was still adjusting.

The front of her sweater felt damp, but at least it didn't show. And the damp patches on the front of her jeans that did show would disappear soon enough. She briskly tightened the ponytail at the back of her head and went back into the nursery, propping her hands on her hips. "What were you saying?"

"What's going to happen next week in court?"

She exhaled. She understood his concern, but she hadn't expected the question quite so soon. "Hasn't Tom Hook explained everything to you?"

Linc inclined his head and set aside the plastic-covered box. "I want to hear it in your words."

She didn't know whether to be touched or not.

She turned around one of the child-size chairs that went with a matching craft table and perched on it. "What happens next week depends on a lot of things. If Layla's mother returns in the meantime, for one."

He snorted softly. "Pardon me if I don't hold my breath. Not even *my* mother would have done what she did."

Maddie wasn't touching that with a ten-foot pole. "Also, if the investigation about her yields anything," she continued. "If you reach Jax or if he returns. If we have the results of both your and Layla's DNA profiles. I'll pick up the court order tomorrow for her test and take her back to the hospital to get that done. You've seen for yourself that it's not going to traumatize her for life or anything." She reached out to slow the swing down a notch.

"A lot of ifs. I don't like a lot of ifs."

"You're in the oil business. Aren't you surrounded by ifs? If this well keeps producing. If it doesn't."

"If I can keep the wolves at bay," he murmured. "All the more reason not to like them."

"What wolves?"

He shook his head. "Judge Stokes said it was too bad I wasn't married. Why? It's not going to even matter when I'm proven to be her uncle."

"Okay. Let's say you are her uncle. That means Jax is her father." Maddie spread her hands. "If he can satisfy Judge Stokes that he wasn't a party to the way she was left with you, then there's no reason I can think of why Layla wouldn't be awarded to him. If he can't prove it, then he'll probably be charged with child endangerment. Neglect at the very least. So will Layla's mother. Whoever she turns out to be."

"Jax wouldn't endanger a child. Not his or anyone else's."

"Well, I don't think so, either." She could see that Layla was nodding off and she turned the setting on the swing even lower. If the baby didn't have a full bottle before she fell asleep, Maddie was going to be in for a long night. She'd learned that in just the past few days. But she was also loath to interrupt the moment with Linc.

So she continued. "But, for the sake of argument, let's suppose that for whatever reason, the judge terminates Jax and Layla's parent-child relationship. That means someone else—you, for instance as her closest responsible relative—could be made her guardian. But nothing is automatic. Not when Layla is already under the protection of the court."

"So even if I'm her uncle, I would have to pass muster."

"Essentially."

"And even if I'm her uncle, I'd pass muster better if I had a wife."

She spread her hands again. "I know it sounds ridiculous, and it *shouldn't* matter. But it does. The court is going to want to place Layla in whatever family situation will best provide for her health and her safety. In a contest between a married couple and a single person, particularly a man—sorry, but that *is* what you are— the married couple usually wins."

"Then I need a wife."

Maddie couldn't stop the short laugh that escaped. "I never pegged you for being dramatic."

"I'm not being dramatic."

Alarm niggled at her insides. "Well, you surely can't be serious!"

His gaze was steady on her face. Uncomfortably so.

She swallowed and strove for reason. "Linc. The only thing you need to be shopping for this week are baby bottles. Certainly not a wife."

"I don't think I'd have to shop far."

Of course, he'd have some female in mind. A man like Linc would naturally have a woman around. Women around.

The alarm spread, running through her veins like some rampant drug, bent on destruction.

"I'm sure you wouldn't," she managed more or less evenly. "Whoever you were out with last Friday night, for instance. But trust me. You don't need to jump that particular gun quite so fast. I mean, what if you're *not* Layla's uncle? Then this is all moot."

"If I'm not, then obviously, I'll need a wife even more."

Her stomach churned. "Why?"

He looked at her, as if it should be obvious. "You said yourself that there weren't any unmarried male foster parents. How else can I make sure Layla could stay here? With me."

"You don't really want a baby." She gestured at Layla. The infant's eyes were closed; she was blissfully unaware of being at the center of so much turmoil. "I can count on one hand the number of times you've actually held her. If she's not your niece, then—"

"You don't know what I want or don't want."

It was like being punched.

Maddie exhaled carefully, knowing that he was right. Aside from what he believed his responsibilities were to Layla, she didn't know anything at all about what he did or didn't want. His ex-wife had been pregnant. This nursery had obviously been built for that child. A child he'd denied having in front of the judge.

If his words were true, was he really simply trying to fill that void?

"Okay," she finally said. "You're saying you want to *keep* Layla?"

"Don't you?"

"Well, yes." The admission came automatically. "But—"

"Then the solution is simple. *You* can marry me."

Her stomach fell away completely. "What?"

"Marry me," he said with inordinate patience.

She scrambled to her feet and the child-size chair tipped over, making a huge racket.

He remained silent. His eyes followed her as she backed away. Though where she thought she would go, she didn't know. Layla was now sound asleep in the swing. She hadn't even started at the chair noise. If Maddie snatched her and took off, the only decent place to go would be her parents' house. And she was too old to be running home to Mom and Dad just because her job was too uncomfortable.

The job's *uncomfortable?*

She stiffened her shoulders, propping her hands on her hips. She'd keep her wits about her if it killed her. "Don't joke. This is too serious."

"Layla's already bonding to you."

"What do *you* know about babies bonding?"

"I know enough. Forget I asked. I made the mistake of thinking you were as interested in her welfare as I am."

She clenched her teeth, feeling dizzy inside from her seesawing emotions. "Up until now, the worst thing you've ever said to me was that Jax and I were bad for each other." She jabbed a finger through the air. "You're the bad one. Suggesting you and I get married? We don't even like each other. Much less feel any of—" she broke off, waving her hand and feeling her face getting hotter by the second "—*that*."

"I'm not suggesting a real marriage," he said evenly. The more uptight she got, the more reasonable he seemed to sound. And it was infuriating. "Just a mutually beneficial arrangement where Layla is concerned. Although you're living in la-la land if you really think there is no—" he waved his hand mockingly "—*that* between us."

The top of her head ought to be smoking, considering the fire burning inside her face. "Go find some other nitwit to fill the bill."

He watched her through narrowed eyes for a long moment. Then—as if her answer really didn't matter all that much, anyway—he shrugged and stood. "That may be some of your best advice yet."

He stepped around the swing and she quickly moved even farther aside.

"Don't worry, Maddie. I'm not my grandfather. I won't ask five times."

Her hands curled into fists. She lifted her chin and made herself meet his eyes. Why would he, when there was no love at all in the asking? All he needed—thought he needed—was a wife for the sake of appearances only. "And I'm not your grandmother. So at least we've got that clear!"

Chapter Ten

By Friday, Maddie didn't need to turn on the lights anymore when she headed downstairs to fix Layla's middle-of-the-night bottles. She'd gotten plenty of practice memorizing the stairs by then.

And fortunately, aside from the night of the marriage "discussion," she hadn't run into Linc during any of her nighttime foraging.

Truthfully, she hadn't run into Linc much at all.

On one hand, it gave her much-needed breathing room.

On the other hand, his absence just made everything worse.

Because if she'd been concerned about his lack of physical interaction with Layla before, it was even more worrying now, the longer it went on.

He left the house at dawn each day. And then he didn't return until Layla was already in bed for the night.

Working a lot? Keeping wolves at bay?

Avoiding the very baby he claimed to want?

Avoiding you?

Out trying to find a nitwit wife?

The noise inside her head was deafening.

Maddie looked down at Layla in the dim light from the pantry while they waited for the bottle to heat.

"He sure hasn't stinted on stuff for you, though," she murmured to the infant. The bottle warmer was state-of-the-art. So was the set of bottles and nipples that went with it. Linc may have been intentionally absent, but he was making certain that Layla had every material thing she could possibly need.

There'd been the warmer and the bottles. A wardrobe fit for a princess. A potty chair that looked like an actual miniature toilet that wasn't necessary, considering how far-off potty training would be. The fancy multi-strapped baby carrier, though?

Maddie bent over the top of Layla's head and dropped a kiss on her sweet-smelling blond hair.

The carrier was definitely spot on the money even though it had taken her several tries and watching a few online videos to get the hang of using it.

Now, instead of having to hold Layla in her arms, she simply strapped her into the soft carrier. Layla got to look out at the world, whether they were the inside the Swift mansion or out in the yard. And Maddie's back didn't get quite so tired as she hefted around a baby that was gaining weight by the day.

She pulled the bottle from the warmer and tested the formula. It was as perfect as the price tag promised and she offered it to the baby. For herself, she broke off half a brownie from the batch she'd made earlier that evening and stuffed it into her mouth. Then she flipped off the pantry light and padded barefoot through the dark kitchen. They went into the living room, but instead of heading straight for the staircase, she lingered in front of the unadorned picture window. It overlooked the long, sloping yard that glimmered whitely beneath the moonlight.

She leaned her head closer to the baby's as they stood by the window. "Your Uncle Linc used to pull me and my sisters on a sled down that hill," she murmured. "Back then, I thought this was the perfect house with the perfect yard." She shifted slightly from side to side, rocking Layla as she drank the bottle. "When you're a little older, maybe he'll take you sledding, too."

She heard a sound and quickly looked over her shoulder.

But she saw nothing except the same dark shapes of furniture. As usual.

"Old houses settle," she told Layla. "That's what I have to remind Ali all the time about our house. It's not ghosts moving things around. It's just the bones of an old house creaking." She rocked her some more. "Maybe we'll go over there tomorrow. See if Auntie Ali and Auntie Greer have agreed on a paint color for the kitchen yet. Shall we make a bet that they haven't?"

"What're the odds?"

She whirled, and Layla protested when she momentarily lost the bottle. Maddie blinked, peering harder into the darkness.

"You don't need to sneak around in your own house," Maddie told Linc, finally making him out sitting in one of the leather wing chairs near the cold fireplace.

"I've been here since you came downstairs." She only realized he had a glass in his hand when he moved his arm and she heard the soft clink of ice. "When you started talking to yourself, I figured I'd better warn you I was here."

"I was talking to Layla." She looked back out the window. The view from the bedroom and nursery upstairs was entirely different—from there, you could see the rear of the house and the stable that, sadly, sat empty these days.

"You make the brownies?"

She wiped her lips, as if he'd caught her with her mouth full. "Yes. Sorry. I kind of made myself at home." Because she'd been going stir-crazy inside his home between endless diapers and bottles and sleepless nights not entirely due to Layla.

"I ate half the pan when I got in a little while ago."

"Kind of late, even for you." She tucked her tongue between her teeth, intending to leave it at that. But of course, to her shame, she couldn't. "Hot date?"

"And if I said yes?"

She made herself shrug, though he probably couldn't make her out any more clearly than she could him. "More power to you," she said blithely. She kept looking out the window. "She know you're in the market for a missus to your mister?"

The ice clinked softly. She heard a faint rustle and felt herself tense as he moved to also stand at the wide window. "You always wanted to sit in the middle of the sled," he said. "Greer in the front. Ali in the back."

"Greer liked to think she was steering. Ali liked to think the back was a wilder ride." She pressed her cheek against Layla's hair, finding that the contact steadied her. "Surprised you remember."

"I remember everything." He lifted his glass and took a sip. Now that he was closer, she could make out the short tumbler and smell the whiskey. "The only happy days we had back then were when we were here with my grandmother."

"I'm glad you were here a lot, then." She chewed the inside of her cheek. "Your grandmother was a really nice woman. My mom always said how much she loved you. You and Jax."

"I know what my dad did. Or tried to do." He took another drink. "Where your mom was concerned. I didn't know back then, but—"

"It doesn't matter," she said quickly. "It was a long time ago."

"If my grandmother knew, she would never have let your mom quit."

"That's why my mother never said anything to Ernestine."

"Instead, she told you?"

"She didn't have to. I used to dust under the foyer table, remember? Not very noticeable to someone who isn't looking."

He absorbed that and swore softly. "Another reason to apologize."

"You're not responsible for what your father did." She sighed faintly. "I didn't even really understand what was happening until later when my mom explained why we weren't coming here so regularly anymore. I don't think your dad ever actually touched her. He just made it too uncomfortable for her with his comments."

"You started coming around again later with Jax."

And by then, Linc had gone away to college. But getting into that period of history was probably not the most sensible thing to do. They'd hashed it over enough, but the results were still the same.

So she changed the subject entirely. "How'd you meet your wife?"

She felt him go still. "Dana?"

"Have you already gotten yourself another one?"

"*Ex*-wife." His voice sounded clipped. "College."

That was what she'd figured. "Love at first sight?"

He lifted his drink again. She could tell his glass was nearly empty just from the sound of the ice. "More like sex at first sight."

She was hardly a prude, but her cheeks turned hot. She pressed one against Layla's head. That's what she got for asking such a question. Being aggravated by the answer was her bad luck. "Sixty-two percent of relationships that start out as sex end up failing."

"You're making that up."

"Entirely."

He let out a short breath. Not a laugh. But more amused than not. "I didn't know your name was really Maude."

It was lobbed from the same left field as her question about his wife. Ex-wife.

"Yes, well, I don't much care for it. It is my legal name. I use it when I need to, but otherwise…" She shrugged. "All my friends know me as Maddie. Greer's got a great name. Ali is really Alicia. Perfectly good name, too."

"Ali fits her better. And you do seem more like a Maddie than a Maude, too."

"I'll take that as a compliment. Our parents named us after some old relatives."

"And Archer?"

"Family name, too. On my dad's side. Archer and Hayley had a different mom. She died when they were little. Then my dad met Meredith, who already had Rosalind."

"Another sister? I don't remember—"

"She grew up in Cheyenne with her father. It was not an easy divorce between my mom and Rosalind's dad. We only got to see her for holidays and a week during summers. She's a lawyer too, though."

"Three lawyers, a cop and a social worker."

"And a psychologist," she reminded. "Don't forget Hayley. I studied psychology, too. Just didn't take it in quite the same direction as she did." Maddie realized that Layla had sucked the bottle dry, so she gently tugged it away. Then she stuffed it in the loose side pocket of her flannel pajama pants and unzipped the fabric carrier to slip Layla out of it.

"What are you doing?"

"I learned the hard way about her burping in this thing." She lifted the baby to her shoulder and firmly patted her back. "Also learned how nicely the carrier turns out after a spin in your washing machine, though." She didn't need to see his face to imagine the grimace he was probably making. "This was a really good purchase," she told him.

"Terry picked it out."

"Ah." She smiled faintly. "I wondered if you'd just opened a website and clicked a buy button or something." Layla burped loudly. "Hurray, sweet pea. And no spit-up. Double hurray."

"She's throwing up?"

"Spitting up," Maddie corrected. "She's not sick. Just getting air with the formula and developing her digestive system. It's normal." She watched him from the corner of her eye. "Would you like to put her back down? She might not sleep as long as I keep hoping, but she does at least fall right back to sleep after her night bottles."

She held her breath when he actually hesitated.

But then he swirled the ice in his glass and took a step away. "She's used to you."

She exhaled. "Linc, she won't get used to *you* unless you give her an opportunity. She's had her poopsplosion for the day and she's not spitting up. You've managed to avoid holding her except for a few occasions. What's the problem?"

"There's no problem."

Layla sighed hugely and curled against Maddie's chest. And oh, how she wished that Linc could experience just how wonderful it felt.

"Does it have something to do with the baby Dana had?"

He didn't answer for a moment. "She didn't have it."

She sighed. "I was afraid it was something like that. You know, sweetie, miscarriages are—"

"She had an abortion. By choice. Her choice."

Maddie's words stopped up in her throat. It wasn't that she was opposed to abortion per se. In fact, she considered herself to be squarely in the pro choice camp. As long as that choice was a responsible one. But Dana had been his *wife*. "I'm sorry," she finally managed.

"It wasn't my child," he said bluntly. "And you don't have to make some big deal about that being why I don't hold Layla."

There were some who thought the history between her parents was a little scandalous. But Meredith and Carter's affair that ultimately produced Maddie and her sisters was nothing in comparison to the stories that just kept coming where Linc's family was concerned.

"Did you know all along that the baby wasn't yours?"

He turned and plunked the glass down on a side table. She thought he wasn't going to answer, particularly when he moved away from the window and headed across the room toward the staircase. "No."

She winced.

And he expected her to believe that his behavior now was unrelated?

She deftly zipped Layla back into the pack—facing toward her this time—and pulled the bottle out of her pocket to leave next to his abandoned glass.

Then she followed him, going up the stairs as quickly as she could without jiggling Layla too much. "When *did* you find out?"

He stopped on the landing and it was a miracle that she didn't bump right into him because of the dark. "I knew it was a mistake to tell you."

"Linc—"

"I found out the baby wasn't mine when I told my brother that Dana was pregnant."

She inhaled sharply. "*Jax* was the baby's father?"

He let out a short, unamused laugh. "That's the irony. When he learned there was going to be a baby, he admitted they'd been sleeping together."

Her shoulders sagged. She couldn't imagine how painful that had to have been.

He was on a roll, though. "But then when we confronted Dana about which one of us *was* the baby's father, it turned out that neither of us was. She was cheating on me with him. And cheating on him with someone else. Just one, big damn sick soap opera with my twisted ex-wife at the center."

Maddie didn't even realize she'd reached for his hand until her fingertips grazed him. "Now I understand why you said you and Jax don't talk much. You probably never forgave—"

Linc turned his hand and squeezed hers briefly, then

let go. "Don't. Don't make so much of this. Jax was as much a sap as I was. More, because he still lets her suck him in whenever she gets bored. He's no saint. He's pulling stunts all the time that cause problems. But he's still my little brother." She felt more than saw him spread his hands. "So. There you have it. The sordid tale of the brothers Swift. We are the logical by-product of Jolene and Blake Swift. Cheaters, one and all."

Maybe Jax was. As friendly as they'd remained over the years, he'd never divulged a word about any of this to Maddie.

What would *she* do if one of her sisters betrayed her so deeply?

The question didn't have an answer. Because she knew that they would never do such a thing.

"So who have you cheated on, Linc?"

His silence felt stoic.

Her heart was pounding so hard it was a wonder that it didn't wake up Layla. Or maybe it was the reason why she was already asleep. The comfort of heavy vibration. Like a truck engine.

"You aren't answering, because there is no answer. You haven't cheated on anyone," she concluded huskily. "It's not in your nature."

"What do you know about my nature?"

"I know more than you think."

"Really?" He suddenly stepped closer.

Every one of Maddie's nerve endings seemed to ripple. And there was still a baby positioned squarely between them.

He lowered his head toward hers.

Her heart beat even faster. She swallowed hard. If he kissed her, she wasn't sure what she would do. Slap him? Ignore him?

Kiss him back?

She moistened her lips.

His head was inches away from hers. His voice seemed to drop an octave. "Am I going to end up having to fight you for Layla?"

"Wha—" She frowned, actually feeling a little dizzy. She took a step back and would have tipped right down the stairs if not for the way he grabbed her arms.

Her heart lodged inside her chest even more tightly as she clutched him in return. "God." Falling on the stairs would be bad enough. With the baby strapped to her chest, it would have been devastating.

"You need a light when you use the stairs."

She felt shaky, but she still managed to shrug off his hold as she moved farther away from the steps.

Kiss him?

As if.

"It's not the lack of light. What do you mean *fight* me for Layla?"

"You said you wanted her, too. The other night."

It had been a thoughtless admission. He hadn't said anything at the time, and she'd hoped he'd forgotten. Or that he hadn't taken any notice.

So much for that idea.

The backs of her eyes burned.

She turned along the hallway and headed toward the nursery. "I would never fight you like that," she said huskily.

"Even if I find the nitwit wife I need?"

She exhaled heavily, annoyance immediately swelling inside her. "For God's sake, Linc. Wasn't one bad marriage enough? You really want to have another? No woman in her right mind would seriously entertain the idea of a marriage of convenience with you! It would never work."

"Why the hell not?"

"Because you're—" She broke off and hurried through the nursery doorway. With the tiny plug-in nightlight, the room felt blindingly bright after the deep darkness in the hallway.

Linc was hard on her heels. He was dressed in dark jeans and an equally dark long-sleeved pullover. Definitely not worn-out pajamas like she was wearing. He looked as dreamy as ever, while she looked like a woman getting three hours of sleep at a stretch because the baby she was caring for wouldn't sleep past that yet.

"I'm what?" He sounded just as annoyed as she felt. "In relatively good health if you don't count the ulcer? Basically house trained?"

She turned on him. "Ulcer?"

"It's an exaggeration." He snatched up the overall-dressed stuffed bear and shook it at her. "I run an oil company for God's sake. Some people actually consider me to be a decent catch."

"It wouldn't matter if you shoveled horse stalls for a living," she said impatiently. "You're still—" she waved her hand expressively at him *"—you."*

He tossed the bear aside. "What the hell is *that* supposed to mean?"

"Shh! You know very well what that means. I hardly need to bolster your tender ego." She quickly unzipped the pack and slid Layla free, depositing her gently into the crib. The baby was wearing one of her new, footed sleepers that kept her perfectly warm without a blanket.

When Layla didn't stir, Maddie turned away from the crib, peeling herself out of the buckles and straps of the fancy baby carrier. She dropped it on top of the changing table and walked into her bedroom.

She wasn't surprised that Linc followed.

She was surprised, however, when he pushed the door closed between the bedroom and the nursery.

She swallowed, abruptly dry-mouthed. The bed behind her was rumpled from her sleeping in it. The clothes she'd worn that day were tossed in a heap on the side chair next to the door. Her lacy bra dangled off the top.

And it was all visible, since she'd left her reading lamp turned on.

She crossed her arms, painfully aware that without the baby carrier strapped all around her torso, the ancient white cami she wore was very thin. Very clinging. And her breasts felt so tight they ached.

"It's late," she said in her best listen-to-me-or-else tone. The one she'd used back in her adult probation days. "We should both be in bed."

His hooded gaze slid toward the bed. He lifted an eyebrow. "Is that an invitation?"

She flushed so hard her face hurt. "No!"

"Pity."

"Do not toy with me, Linc. I'm in no mood."

"You're the last person I'd toy with," he assured her. "You're pretty much holding what I want right in your pretty little hands."

She closed her eyes and raked her fingers through her hair, wanting to pull it right out. "How many times do I have to tell you that *I* am not the one who'll decide anything where Layla is concerned?" She released her hair and it tumbled around her face, the ponytail holder failing completely. "All I can do is make sure she's taken care of and still keep her accessible to you while I can!"

"*That's* why you put yourself out on the chopping block the way you did?"

Why, oh why couldn't she have just heated up Layla's bottle and brought her back upstairs to feed her?

Why did she have to go into the living room? Why did he have to be in there the way he had been?

He didn't like so many what ifs.

She didn't like so many whys.

She pushed the hair out of her eyes, not looking at him. Just once, she'd like to feel like she was at her very best around him. That she was at the top of her game. "If I tell you yes, will you leave me alone?"

"Is it the truth?"

She sighed. "Yes, it's the truth. In case you never noticed, I'm a terrible liar."

"I noticed."

Of course he had.

She walked over to the door that led into the hallway and opened it. Even he wouldn't be able to ignore the message. "Good night, Linc."

His jaw flexed. He moved to the doorway, towering over her the way he always did.

When he lifted his hand and touched her chin, pushing it upward, she froze. Kept her lashes lowered.

"What am I going to do with you?"

Something inside her ached. "You could try to make me go away like you did before. But that would mean Layla goes with me."

"Not everything is about Layla."

At that, she did lift her lashes. She looked up at him. "Now who's a bad liar?"

His lips thinned.

She lifted her chin away from his fingers. She pulled the door open even wider, clinging to the knob because she honestly wasn't sure that her shaking knees would hold her up. "Right now, everything is about Layla. There is not one single thing you could do or say to make me believe otherwise."

His gaze roved over her face. Looking for what, she couldn't say. But it left her feeling almost as raw as that damned artificial tree of Ali's had.

"Then I guess there's nothing else to say but goodnight," he finally said.

He stepped through the doorway, leaving the small circle of light cast from her reading lamp. She still kept watch until he wasn't even a shadowy shape in the dark hall.

Only then did she finally close the bedroom door and lean back weakly against it.

Chapter Eleven

"Svelte Sage." Looking triumphant, Ali waved the paint chip in front of Maddie. "Greer and I both love it. She gave her vote of approval before she went into work, not even thirty minutes ago."

Maddie blearily eyed the color sample. It was vaguely green. Vaguely gray. Vaguely brown. It was also the one she'd chosen a week ago. "Looks fine."

"It's better than fine. When the cabinets are done in off-white, it'll look spectacular." Ali peered into Maddie's face. "I thought you'd be more enthusiastic."

Ali had greeted her with the sample practically the second she'd walked into the house.

Maddie sank down on the couch, one arm around Layla, who was once more strapped in the fabric carrier. "I'm thrilled," she assured her sister. "Maybe when we actually have the kitchen finished—" in the next millennium, hopefully "—I'll be even more thrilled." She hooked the toe of her boot around the coffee table and dragged it a little closer so that she could prop her feet on it. Once Linc had left her bedroom the night before, it had been hours before she'd finally fallen asleep. Only to be awakened a short while later by Layla, yet again.

"You're exhausted is what you are," Ali said tartly. She nudged Maddie's legs to one side and sat on the coffee table. "You look like death warmed over."

"Thank you *so* much." Then she promptly yawned.

"How much partying are you doing over there with our resident oilman?"

She closed her eyes and leaned her head back against the couch. Layla wasn't asleep, but she was perfectly content sitting the way she was in front of Maddie. "I've, uh, actually hardly seen him." She mentally crossed her fingers. "It doesn't feel as cold here as I expected it to be."

"There was frost on the *inside* of the windows last night. Just in case you're considering leaving the swell Swift digs." Ali wiggled Maddie's shin. "Sit up. Take off that contraption you're wearing. I'll watch Layla for an hour and *you* can take a nap. Or a shower. Either one would be an improvement."

Maddie peeled open her gritty eyes. "It's so nice to be able to count on such sisterly support."

"I said I'd watch Layla," Ali countered. "That's pretty supportive if you ask me."

"Only if you change her diaper when she actually needs it." Maddie sat up with an effort and undid the carrier, working the infant out of it. "You ought to try it," she told Ali. "Makes carrying her a lot easier."

"Well, for now, I'll pass on the straitjacket." Ali lifted Layla onto her lap, kissing her cheek and neck so noisily that the baby chortled. "God, I love that sound." She shoved Maddie's shoulder. "Now, for the love of God, *go*."

"I had a shower yesterday," Maddie groused as she headed toward the stairs.

"Did you actually turn on the water?"

She rolled her eyes, ignoring Ali. The truth was, though, that her shower had probably lasted all of three minutes. Because that was about how much time Layla had allowed her.

She passed Greer's open bedroom door and was momentarily tempted to use her bathtub. But if she actually laid down in a soaking tub filled with hot, bubbly water, she wasn't sure she'd ever want to get out.

So the shower it was.

Maddie's barebones bathroom was colder than a witch's glare. But she turned on the space heater she dragged in there and let the shower steam fill the air. It got so cozy that when she stepped under the hot spray and let it sluice over her, she might actually have nodded off and napped right there, still standing up.

How did mothers everywhere manage to care for infants day in and day out without help? Even though Maddie was a qualified foster-care provider, she'd never had a three-month-old. She'd had a three-week-old once. The baby had slept and ate and pooped. But mostly slept. She'd had a three-year-old, too, who slept solidly through the night, thirteen hours straight. There'd been others over the years, but never for more than a few days at a time.

She and Layla were now on day eight.

Only the fear of running out of hot water made her lethargic limbs finally move. She washed her hair. Twice. Shaved her legs. Twice. When she finally shut off the water and climbed out into the steam-shrouded bathroom, she felt cleaner than she had in a week. Most of her toiletries were at Linc's, but she found an old comb and managed to work out the tangles in her hair before twisting it into a braid.

Then, still wrapped in the bath towel, she went into the bedroom and crawled under the covers.

An hour. One entire blissful hour, she told herself. With no thoughts of Linc allowed.

She closed her eyes. In seconds she was asleep.

And dreaming about Linc.

"Well, there's Sleeping Beauty finally."

Maddie smiled ruefully and padded into the kitchen wearing her one pair of flannel-lined jeans and a thick red sweater. "You let me sleep too long," she told Ali. "But I see you discovered the miracle that is the baby carrier."

Ali grinned. She was standing at the sink washing dishes, wearing Layla in front of her. The baby was obviously happy to be up close and personal with the occasional soapsud that found its way to her. "This thing is great," she agreed. "Once I figured out how all the straps and buckles worked I could carry this little girl all day long, I think."

"She'd let you." Maddie found a mug and filled it with the cold coffee that was still in the coffeemaker. She stuck it in the microwave to heat it up. "She *much* prefers to be held than not. She has made that perfectly clear to me." She leaned over and kissed the baby on her head. "Haven't you, sweet pea?"

Layla gave her a smile that made Maddie feel good all the way to her toes.

Ali wasn't smiling, though. She was watching her

with narrowed eyes. "She's not going to be so easy to give up, is she?"

"She's not mine to give up. Remember?" The microwave dinged and she took out the mug. The liquid was lukewarm, but she routinely drank worse at the office, so it would do just fine.

"Do *you* remember?" Ali's gaze was steady. "Really?"

Maddie swallowed.

"Oh, Maddie," Ali sighed. "This is what you do. You get too involved."

"This is different."

Her sister lifted an eyebrow. But she withheld comment and rinsed another dish and placed it in the plastic drainer. Then she pulled the plug and watched the sink drain from below where the pipes were visible thanks to the unfinished, doorless cabinetry.

"What are you doing?"

"It's been leaking this week." Ali snatched a soup pot, quickly stuck it under the pipes, and then covered Layla's ears. "Another damn thing to fix." She shot Maddie a look. "Do *not* tell Dad."

"If you could keep your ghosts from moving the tools, I can probably change out the pipes. Ray and I did it once for a family we were helping."

"Didn't know that plumbing was part of the job description in family services."

Maddie carried her coffee over to the table and sat. "When it comes to family services, a varied skill-set is the name of the game. And sometimes you have to get involved."

You can marry me.

She pinched the bridge of her nose, willing away

Linc's voice. She was not considering it. "Not that involved," she muttered.

"What?" Ali was looking at her.

"Nothing." Maybe sleeping three hours had been too long. Maybe it had turned her brain to mush. "Did you feed Layla?"

"Yup. She sucked down all eight ounces of one of those bottles you had in the diaper bag. Fancy bag, too. Quite the step up from that purse you were using."

"Linc got it. What about her diaper? You have checked it, haven't you?"

"No, I took her to the neighbor to do it." Ali rolled her eyes. "Yes. She peed twice. Fortunately, just pee, else your nap would have been shortened to deal with it. Relax, would you?"

"Sorry." Maddie propped her chin on her hand. Her sister was dressed similarly to her, though she'd pinned her hair on top of her head. most likely to keep it away from Layla's grasping hands. "How've things been at work this week?"

"Pretty much the same. Sarge remains pissed off at me. So he's still assigning me every crap detail he can." Her sister shrugged. "It'll blow over eventually. Fortunately, he hasn't blocked me out from everything concerning Layla. I know there haven't been any recent reports of a missing baby at least."

"What about the note? Do you know if anything's being done about it?"

"I know it's written on paper that can be bought in nearly any store. How's life with Linc?"

Despite her best efforts, Maddie could feel her face warm. "I told you earlier, we rarely see him. He works a lot."

"So why do you look like you've been caught with your hand down his cookie jar?"

"Ali!"

"That's what this is really about. Not just a sweet little baby. You're falling for him, aren't you?"

"I'm not falling for Lincoln Swift!"

The back door opened just then and their mother hurried inside, slowing only long enough to make sure that Vivian, who was following her, made it in safely, too.

"Don't coddle me," Vivian said a little testily as she shrugged off Meredith's hand. She was almost as petite as Meredith, who was only five feet tall. "I'm old. Not dead. At least not yet."

"Don't joke," Meredith chided. Because it wasn't a joke. Vivian Archer Templeton, on the high side of her eighties, had an inoperable brain tumor. So far, it was just "squatting" as Vivian liked to say. But they all knew that anything was possible. Nothing could happen with it. Or everything could happen with it.

Needless to say, they all hoped for the nothing end of that particular spectrum.

Vivian made an impatient sound. But there was still a gleam of affection in her dark brown eyes as she looked at her daughter-in-law. "Better to joke than to run around morose all the time." She patted her stylish silver hair as she surveyed the deplorable state of the kitchen. "Would you *please* let me get this place finished for you?"

Meredith had spotted Layla and was greedily slipping the baby out from the carrier. "Watch your hair, Mom," Maddie warned. Then she looked back at her grandmother. "We are not letting you pay for our refurbishing." It was an old argument. "Want me to take your coat?" It was a fancy fur. Real, no doubt.

"No thank you, dear." Vivian sat at the table, giving Maddie's mug of coffee an appraising look. "We've just come from lunch and won't be long. Here." She pulled a bundle of red yarn from her pocket. "Your mother told me about the baby."

Maddie shook out the bundle. It was a baby-size knitted cap. "Did *you* knit it?"

"Good Lord, no." Vivian looked appalled at the very idea. "You should put it on her head, though. It's very chilly in here. I suppose you've noticed."

Maddie and Ali shared a look. "You could say that."

"Meredith, your daughters are as stubborn as that son of mine you married."

"Yes they are, Vivian," Meredith returned equably. She was cuddling the baby, who had, despite the warning, wrapped her little hands in Meredith's long dark ringlets. She might be in her fifties now, but their mom had more hair than all three of the triplets combined. She also got along a lot better with her mother-in-law than Carter did. "I can't believe this is Ernestine's greatgranddaughter."

"*Possibly* her great-granddaughter," Maddie corrected. "We still don't have proof."

"All I've heard about it is bits and pieces. How is Linc?"

Maddie didn't dare look at her mother. "Fine." She buried her nose in the dreadful coffee.

Vivian toyed with the rings on her fingers. "He's a handsome one, that Lincoln Swift."

"He mentioned you've met," Maddie mumbled.

"If I were thirty years younger—"

"You'd still be too old for him," Meredith said, laughing.

"True. And handsome or not, I could never do better than my dear Arthur." He'd been the last of her four husbands, and to hear her tell it, the great love of her life, even though she still used the name she'd gotten when she'd married Carter's father. She looked at Ali and Maddie. "I expect both of you to bring suitable escorts to my party next week."

"You'll be lucky if I arrive wearing a suitable dress," Ali warned, not in the least bit cowed.

"What about you?" Vivian caught Maddie's eye.

"I, uh, I'll borrow something from Hayley again." She would need to remember to call her about it.

"And an escort?"

"Archer will do."

Vivian sniffed derisively. "He's your brother. He should be bringing a woman of his own."

Ali grinned. "He'd have to throw dice to choose just one."

"Is that why you dropped by?" Maddie had become very fond of her grandmother over the past year. But she wasn't oblivious to Vivian's attitudes. Admittedly, she'd made a lot of progress since moving from Pennsylvania, but she was nevertheless a duck out of water. Caviar and diamonds among cowboy beans and boots. "To make sure we don't embarrass you at your party?"

"What would a good party be without someone getting a little embarrassed by something? You'll bring Lincoln Swift."

"I will?"

"You like him, don't you? I hear you're staying under his roof."

"That's temporary. And strictly because of the baby."

Vivian waved her hand, looking unsettlingly crafty. "Bring him anyway. He'll be an interesting addition to our evening."

"I can't just drag him to a party, Vivian."

"Maybe you can ask Morton," Ali suggested slyly.

Meredith glanced up from Layla. "Who's Morton?"

"Nobody," Maddie assured her. "Nobody at all."

"I knew a Morton once," Vivian reflected. "Pillar of salt, he was."

Despite herself, Maddie laughed. She glanced at her mother, and wished she hadn't. Meredith was watching her with a knowing look.

Mrs. Lincoln Swift.

She quickly looked back at her coffee. She wasn't seventeen anymore, doodling dreamily on a school notebook. "So, anyone going to the Glitter and Glow parade tonight?"

"I tried talking your father into it. So far, he's refusing," Meredith replied. "Says he's already put in his time sitting out in the cold watching crazies wearing Christmas lights when you girls were growing up."

"He'll give in. He always does when it comes to you. Which is why he's there, every year, watching the crazies. As for me, I'll be working, keeping the peace among them." Ali plucked the pencil out of her hair and fluffed it out around her shoulders. "What do you all think of me trying to go blond?"

"I think you should concentrate your efforts on this house and let your hair alone," Meredith said dryly. She handed the baby to Maddie. "Vivian, I'd better get you back to Weaver before they start closing off streets for the parade and make it impossible to reach the highway."

"You didn't drive yourself to Braden?" Maddie asked. Vivian had an ostentatious Rolls Royce that she tended to drive like a maniac. "Are you feeling all right?"

"I'm fine," Vivian assured her blithely. "The Rolls is simply having a tune-up."

In Vivian-speak, Maddie knew that could mean anything from an oil change to dent removal.

"Maybe we'll see you at the parade," Meredith said as they left. "Bring Linc. Ernestine used to take him and Jax every year." She closed the door after Vivian.

Maddie exhaled. She worked the cap over Layla's head. The baby immediately began trying to pull it back off.

"Remember when life used to be uncomplicated?" She looked at Ali.

"Yeah," Ali said wryly. "Me, either."

The Glitter and Glow parade ran through the center of Braden every year. From his upstairs bedroom, Linc could probably see the lights of it if he'd wanted to.

Maddie and Layla had been gone all day. She'd left the house early that morning and still been gone when he came home after spending the day on conference calls with his lawyers and the folks at OKF.

If it weren't for the clothes that were still lying in a pile in the bedroom, he would have been certain that she didn't intend to bring the baby back. That *she* didn't intend to come back.

But what were a few pairs of jeans and a hank of lace, anyway? She'd told him that first night that Layla's needs were basic. Maybe Maddie's were equally basic. Maybe she didn't care about leaving the clothes behind, if it meant she didn't have to put up with Linc anymore.

He exhaled heavily and turned away from the window.

Jax's phone was sitting on his dresser. He'd kept it charged, even though he still hadn't figured out the password. And he could tell that multiple messages had been coming in even though he couldn't access them.

He swiped across the photo of the sailboat blonde and jabbed in some random numbers, as unsuccessfully as all the others he'd tried. What he needed was a phone hacker. Unfortunately, Linc didn't happen to have such a person on his speed dial.

He left the phone where it was and went down the hall. The nursery—even full of stuff—was neater than Maddie's bedroom. He picked up one of the sleepers that were folded on top of the changing table. The elf-looking one. It was so tiny.

He'd gotten over Jax and Dana. As much as he ever would, anyway. But this—

He crumpled the sleeper in his fist.

He heard a wail from downstairs and dropped it, striding out into the hall. From the head of the stairs, he watched Maddie juggle the baby and the diaper bag and the house key as she entered the house.

She was home.

The relief was almost more than he could stand.

He closed his hand tightly over the newel post. "Where the hell have you been all day?" *Good one, Linc. Just piss her off right from the start.*

Her head jerked back as she looked up the staircase, her dark hair gleaming beneath the chandelier. "We spent the day with Ali." Her voice was cool as she unwrapped the blanket around Layla and shrugged out of her coat. "Where the hell have *you* been all day?"

"Same place I've been all week. Keeping my father from selling Swift Oil out from under us all."

Layla was still crying, but Maddie went stock-still, looking up at him. "Are you serious?"

He unlocked his grip and started down the stairs. "Is she hungry or something?"

"Since she's always hungry, I'm guessing yes." Maddie dumped her coat on the bottom stair alongside the diaper bag. "Unfortunately, I didn't plan for her to go through as many bottles as she did today. Either that, or Ali was drinking formula behind my back." She headed into the kitchen, stopping short when she spotted the high chair that had been delivered that day. "Linc." She looked over her shoulder as he followed her. "How much more stuff are you planning to buy for her?"

"As much as she needs."

"Then I guess you better not let Swift Oil get sold out from under you." She sidestepped the high chair that he'd positioned near the island and carried the baby into the pantry. She came out a second later with the can of powdered formula.

He took it from her. "I'll do it."

Her lashes swept down, but not soon enough to hide the surprise in her eyes. While he quickly grabbed a clean bottle and started filling it, she tried distracting Layla with the usual wooden spoon, but the baby wasn't having any of it. The only thing that quieted her was the bottle when he finally handed it to Maddie.

She slid onto one of the barstools and held the baby on her lap to feed her. "So how serious is this thing with your father? Really."

"Couple hundred million dollars' worth of serious." Linc grimaced. "I'm buying him out."

She looked shocked. "Just like that." She snapped her fingers.

"It's a little more complicated than that, but essentially. Money's what matters to my father, so money's what he'll get."

"And Jax? Doesn't he have any say?"

"If he were here in the first place, it wouldn't even be necessary. I wouldn't have to sell off some of my own holdings just to keep the entire damned company safe."

"My brain doesn't even understand numbers that high," she murmured. "I don't know why I keep forgetting that you're rich."

"Not as rich as I was when I woke up this morning. And fortunately, my lawyers do understand."

She was silent for a moment, looking down at Layla. She tenderly smoothed the baby's hair that looked blonder than ever against the dark red sweater Maddie wore. Then she seemed to take a deep breath. "Justin called me when we were on our way back here," she said quickly. "Your DNA profile is finished."

His muscles tightened. "And?"

"And nothing. Layla's test isn't complete yet."

He almost wished she hadn't told him. His stomach burned and he grabbed the milk from the fridge.

"He said he'd let me know the second they're able to compare them."

"Before the hearing on Tuesday?"

She was chewing her lip. "I don't know. Maybe."

He swore under his breath. "Give me lawyers and my old man any day of the week." He flipped the cap off the glass milk bottle and drank straight from it. When he finally capped it again, Maddie was watching him.

Her eyes were dark. "If you have an ulcer, you shouldn't have been drinking whiskey last night."

"I don't have an ulcer." He grimaced. "I *did*, but it's healed."

She raised an eyebrow, looking pointedly at the milk.

"Call it prevention." He shoved the bottle back into

the fridge. "We need to take her to the parade," he said abruptly.

Her mouth rounded slightly. "It's already started. That's why it took me so long to get here. Trying to navigate around all the closed-off streets."

"I still want her to see it."

"She's only three—" Maddie shrugged. "Okay." She slid off the barstool. "Bring the formula. Just in case."

He grabbed the canister and the only clean bottle sitting in the rack and shoved them into the diaper bag.

"Where are we going to watch from? The stroller's in my trunk." She wrapped Layla into a tiny white coat.

He hadn't even known they made coats for babies her size.

"She seems to prefer the carrier, though." Maddie was still talking as she maneuvered her arms into her own coat while still holding the bundled baby and the bottle. "Can't say I blame her. Body contact and all. She shouldn't really know that she was left the way she was, but who is to say for sure?" She flipped her hair out from the collar of her coat and glanced up at Linc.

Everything about her seemed to still, except for those deep, expressive eyes. "What?"

He stepped closer. Leaned down and kissed her.

She gave a startled jerk, followed immediately by the heady softening of her lips. Followed just as immediately by her hand on his chest, shoving him away.

Then she scrambled from him for good measure, clutching the baby against her. Even Layla was giving him a wide-eyed look, momentarily disinterested in the bottle that Maddie had also seemed to forget. "What on earth are you thinking?"

That she was right. A marriage of convenience had been a stupid idea. "That you should marry me before

Tuesday. Then when we get to court next week, it'll be a done deal."

She turned away from him, giving the bottle once more to the baby. "You're out of your tree."

"We both want Layla."

"Linc—"

"And I want you."

She froze. "You're only saying that because of the situation."

"The situation being that you turn me on the same way you always have?"

She huffed. Her cheeks flushed. "Cut it out. You're just panicking."

"Over...?"

"You know. The DNA test being done. The hearing getting closer. The—"

"—fact that you were gone the entire day and I wasn't sure you'd come back?"

She blinked. Layla blinked.

Then Maddie cleared her throat. "As long as the judge lets me keep Layla, I'm not going anywhere," she said huskily. "Just, um, just stop proposing."

"Or what?"

Her lips compressed. Her eyes were suddenly filled with ire. "Or I might accept just to spite you. And *then* where would we be?"

In bed, he thought immediately.

Fortunately, he managed to have the good sense not to say it.

Chapter Twelve

"What do you think?"

Maddie stared up at the enormous tree. "I think it's probably illegal to cut down a tree like this."

Linc's smile flashed. "Not if I own the land it's on."

It was Sunday morning and they were standing in the middle of nowhere. All because Maddie had evidently lost her mind where Linc was concerned.

It wasn't even the proposals, which she resolutely refused to take seriously. Yes, she'd lost all hope of objectivity where Layla and Linc were concerned. But she hadn't lost every shred of her common sense. And common sense dictated there were solutions to be found that didn't involve saying vows that weren't true.

No, it wasn't the proposals.

It wasn't even the kiss that had rocked her back on her heels despite its brevity.

It was the parade.

And the fact that Linc had found a spot, right on the curb in front of the Swift Oil office, where they'd sat and watched all of the cars and trucks and even people, wrapped in Christmas lights, progress along the street while Christmas carols played from loudspeakers, sometimes warring with the high school band and the choral groups who passed.

It was the fact that he'd plucked Layla out of Maddie's arms and held her up so she could see over the kids sitting on the ground in front of them.

It was the fact that he'd finally, *finally*, had a smile on his face.

The kind of smile that he used to have.

The kind of smile that he was giving her now.

He had mirrored sunglasses on his face and a chainsaw in his gloved hand and he used it to point at the tree again. "Well?"

She glanced back at the truck. Layla was in her car seat, safely strapped inside. She'd fallen asleep before they'd even gotten outside of town. She hadn't stirred a muscle since.

Maddie waved her arm and tried to pretend she didn't feel all warm and gooey inside every time she looked his way. "This isn't an oil field." There hadn't been a single pump jack or derrick in miles. The snowy hillside where he'd driven them was more suited to a ski run. Their only stop on the hour-long drive had been at a dinky café also in the middle of nowhere. But the delicious coffee and breakfast sandwiches explained the surprising number of vehicles that had been parked outside of it. "How do I trust that you actually own it?"

He made a point of patting the pockets of his down jacket. "Sorry. I must have left the deed in my other coat." He extended one long arm. "This is the same hillside where my grandmother always got her tree. *Her* tree. Because Gus planted all of these firs for her about a million years ago. So, yes or no?"

"If I say no, you're going to drag us around looking at every tree here, aren't you."

He considered it. "Maybe."

Maddie couldn't help but laugh. If anyone had told her even twenty-four hours ago that they'd be standing together this way, knee-deep in snow, she'd have said that *they* were the ones who'd lost their minds.

But it was just her.

Mindless Maddie.

"How long has it been since you've had a Christmas tree?"

"I don't know. Long time. Before college. You gonna keep asking questions or pick a tree?"

"Pick," she said, nodding toward the tree in question. "It's perfect."

He started toward it. "Get back in the truck." He braced the back of the saw against his leg and gave a pull on the start cord. The chainsaw whirred to life with a low rumble.

Then he hit the throttle a few times, and it growled louder.

It was stupid. But she felt a visceral jolt deep inside her when he easily swung the heavy-duty saw around to the base of the tree.

It didn't take him long. It was over almost as quickly as it began. The chainsaw buzzed, chips of bark flew, and a moment later, Linc was pushing the tree away from him. It fell, almost in slow motion, its deep bluish green branches sending up a cloud of snow when it hit the ground.

He killed the chainsaw, then leaned down and

grabbed the base of the tree and started dragging it back toward her.

All manly, manly man.

God help her.

"Told you to get in the truck," he said when he neared.

"You should know by now that I don't always listen well." It was better to stay active than stand there drooling, so she lowered the tailgate herself and moved around the tall tree to help him lift it into the bed. She wasn't much help. She barely grabbed a few branches before he'd shoved the tree into the bed. Since it had to be at least twelve feet tall, it stuck out well beyond the tailgate.

"Close the gate when I lift it, would you?"

She scrambled under the tree, squinting against the heady scent.

"You're not going to end up with another rash, I hope." He lifted the tree.

She nimbly closed the gate and popped back out from beneath the tree. "Never have before." She brushed a few needles out of her hair. "It's the artificial stuff that got me. Ali's been on a tear about the fire hazards of real trees or we'd have had one ourselves."

"Yeah, well, this thing is so fresh, it'll be good until February." He unwound a bundle of rope and tossed it over the tree. She grabbed the end and went up on her toes to reach inside the bed, her gloved fingers searching. His boots crunched on the snow as he came around to her side. He gave her a surprised look when he realized she'd already looped the rope through the tie-down.

"Come on," she said. "Just because we were girls didn't mean my dad made us sit in the truck staying all pretty and clean every time we went out for fire-wood and stuff."

He smiled faintly and threw the rope back across the tree, then headed around to the far side of the truck. "No cutting your own Christmas trees?"

"Always picked them from one of the lots in town." She caught the rope again when it headed her way. "My mother always opts for the scraggliest one—you know the one. The Charlie Brown tree. 'Cause she figures it needs more love. My dad always likes the fattest." She closed her eyes, feeling along the inside of the truck bed for the next tie-down. Linc had a fancy bed liner, so it wasn't quite what she was used to. "Which tree did we always end up with?" Her fingertip finally found the notch and she quickly slithered the long rope through it. "The scraggly one. Because my father has never been able to say no to my mom. They're still besotted with each other. It was embarrassing when we were kids."

"And now?"

She tossed the rope over the tree, missing by a long shot. But he still managed to snag the rope and pull it across. "Now?" It was what she wanted. What they all wanted. "Catching your parents making out?" she said with a tart laugh. "Still embarrassing."

He sent the rope back her way. "Better than finding them making out with other people." His voice was dry.

"Well, that's true."

Between the two of them, they quickly had the tree secured beneath the crisscrossing rope. The branches would still blow a lot when they got back on the highway—no way to prevent it—but the tree was definitely not going anywhere they didn't want it to go.

Then Linc stored the chainsaw in the bed, too, and they got back inside the truck.

Layla had slept the entire while.

"Sure," Maddie murmured as she leaned over the back of her seat to adjust the blanket over the baby. "You can't sleep three hours straight at night, but when it's daylight?" She lightly brushed the red cap on Layla's head and then pushed herself back into her own seat. She felt a little breathless and she loosened her coat and pulled off her gloves before fastening her seatbelt.

Linc was just sitting there, watching her.

"Don't tell me you're out of gas," she warned. But of course, she knew they weren't. The truck had been running the entire while they'd been messing with the tree.

"I should have hired you some help with Layla."

She gaped at him, then shook her head, trying not to feel as flustered as he made her. "I *am* the help, remember?" She gestured at the windshield. "Come on. Get moving. There's a tree yet to be decorated."

He put the truck in gear and slowly turned until he was lined up once more with the tracks they'd made in the snow on their way there. "There's nothing wrong with my memory and you cleared me up once on that point. You're not a babysitter."

"Yeah, well, that's when I thought the reason you called me was to get Layla off your hands." Which seemed a lot longer ago than it really had been.

She realized she was staring at his hands. He'd taken off his gloves, too. His fingers were lightly wrapped around the steering wheel.

"So." She swallowed, looking away. "I hope you kept your grandmother's tree ornaments. Otherwise we'll be stringing a lot of popcorn to get that sucker covered."

"Should be in the attic. I didn't get rid of anything of hers. Just moved a few things around to make room for some new."

Of course he hadn't. "New like your den."

"Home office. Master bedroom. Much as I appreciate my grandmother's antiques, I draw the line at the dinky beds."

Red flashing lights of danger there. Maddie did not need to be thinking about his bedroom. Much less his bed.

So, of course, she did. His room was at the very end of the hall. She'd learned that much over the past week. It was several doors down from hers.

Seven doors, to be exact.

She chewed the inside of her cheek, blindly studying the landscape outside her window.

"Marry me and you could make whatever changes you wanted. Even choose a scraggly tree next year."

She shot him a look.

He shrugged, looking anything but innocent. "Just sayin'."

She exhaled noisily and looked out the side window again.

And she absolutely did *not* feel a smile tugging at her lips.

Four hours later, the tree was standing tall and stately next to the staircase.

Linc had dragged two boxes of ornaments down from the attic and a ladder up from the basement.

It was obvious at first glance the ornament boxes hadn't been opened in quite some time. Probably not since his grandmother died.

She'd vowed right then and there to make certain every single item got placed on the tree. Even the popsicle-stick ones that were in major danger of falling apart as soon as she touched them.

She was wearing Layla in the fabric carrier. At Linc's

request, she'd made another batch of homemade brownies. She'd added hot chocolate to the menu. And Christmas music.

With the snowflakes blowing around outside the windows, they probably looked like a very normal family enjoying the holiday season.

But they weren't normal.

And they weren't a family.

And it was more than a little worrisome that she had to keep reminding herself of that fact.

"Here." She reached into the box and pulled out a wooden nutcracker. The paint on it was faded. Layla reached for it, but Maddie avoided the little grasping hands, giving it to Linc where he stood on the ladder. "Only thing that's left in the box is the star." She bent down and retrieved it, too, pulling the silver and white tree topper carefully from its protective nest of shredded paper. Layla grabbed at it and promptly started crying when Maddie held it out of her reach. "Sorry, baby." She brushed her lips against Layla's cheek. "This one's not for you, either."

"Should have got some rattles for her to hang," Linc said, stepping down the ladder. "Here, give her to me."

Maddie stared. Then she hurriedly set down the star next to their cocoa mugs and unzipped the pack, working Layla out of it.

The baby kicked, almost squirming out of Maddie's hands, but she held fast until Linc took her.

Layla looked as surprised as Maddie felt when he lifted the baby up to look into her face.

She kicked a few more times.

She stopped crying.

Then she gave him a few gurgling sounds that

quickly developed into her distinctive chortle that charmed Maddie every single time she heard it.

He wasn't immune, either. She could tell by the way he grinned.

He adjusted his hold on the infant, tucking her against his chest, and stepped up the ladder with her. "Hand me the star."

Maddie sucked in her lip. One part of her wanted to warn him to be careful on the ladder with the baby.

The other part wanted to savor the moment forever.

She handed him the star.

He went up two more rungs.

She quickly dragged her phone out of her pocket and snapped a picture of him as he reached up to put the star in place on top of the tree.

"How's it look?"

She swallowed the knot in her throat and slid her phone away before he could see. The star was listing slightly to one side. Layla was grabbing for the nearest thing, which happened to be Linc's shirt collar. "It's perfect," she said huskily.

He came down the ladder and looked up to survey his handiwork. "You need glasses."

She laughed softly, shaking her head. She handed him a brownie. "Don't argue. I said it was perfect."

Then he smiled, too. "Okay. It's perfect." He wolfed the brownie in two bites and dropped his arm over her shoulders as he looked again at the tree. "My grandmother would have liked it," he said after a moment.

Her chest tightened. "Yeah." It was all she could manage. She shifted, enough for the casual arm around her shoulders to fall away. She could breathe easier, but did she really want to? "I, uh, I should probably fix us something more substantial to eat than brownies."

He took the last one from the plate and grabbed her wrist, looking at her watch. "A little early for dinner, isn't it?"

She retrieved her tingling arm and needlessly adjusted her watchband. "Not when there's an infant in the house who needs bathing and rocking before she'll even entertain the idea of sleep."

He considered that. "I don't usually eat much here."

"I noticed. Aside from baby formula, your pantry was mostly shelf-paper and saltines."

"So how'd you make the brownies?"

"Wiggling my nose? We shopped, obviously." She picked up the plate and the mugs and carried them into the kitchen, leaving him still holding Layla.

"You shouldn't have done that." He'd followed her.

"Well. It's done. You have peanut butter on your pantry shelf now." She turned on the faucet to rinse out the mugs. "Live with it."

"I'll take you out to dinner."

She nearly dropped the crockery in the sink. "That's not necessary."

"Not for you, maybe. But how do I know you can cook? Brownies aside—"

"Oh, nice! Just for that, you deserve to buy me dinner. An expensive one." She shut off the water and flicked her wet fingers at him. Layla laughed and bumped her head against Linc's chin. "Layla agrees."

"Expensive restaurant." He narrowed his eyes in exaggerated thought. "In Braden."

"Okay. So maybe not expensive. But not takeout." She slid Layla out of his hold. "We want proper sit-down with table service. Isn't that right, Layla?"

The baby batted her blue eyes and gave her gummy smile.

Then, because it was feeling much, much too homey standing in his kitchen together, Maddie forced herself to move away.

"Where are you going now?"

She gave him a quick grin that hopefully masked her odd breathlessness. "Young ladies of a certain age need to dress properly for every occasion. Particularly those of the three-ish month range who have a drawer full of pretty things with their price tags still on."

"So much for the proper dress," Linc said a few hours later when he came into the nursery to find Layla in the middle of a diaper change. He made a face and took a step back toward the doorway. "What's *in* that stuff she drinks?"

Maddie chuckled and finished wiping Layla's tiny little butt. "Wonderful nourishment. And trust me. This is better than it'll be when she starts eating pizza like what we just had." She twisted up the soiled diaper and wipes and nudged her toe against the diaper pail. The lid popped up and she dropped it inside. She left the lid to close automatically and picked up the naked baby.

"You don't put 'em out in the garbage?"

What happened to the manly manly-man? "You are *such* a priss," she accused on a laugh as she went into the bathroom. "You bought the diaper pail!"

"Terry—"

"Yeah, yeah. Your receptionist and gatekeeper. I know." She leaned over and turned on the water and while it warmed, grabbed the usual stack of towels. "Just warning you now that you'd better put Terry on a budget where choosing stuff for Layla is concerned, or one day you'll have a very spoiled little girl on your hands." She went down on her knees alongside the tub and tucked a towel between Layla's rear and her jeans. Just in case.

He'd moved to the doorway. He was standing on the threshold, his boots close, but not crossing it. "Got enough towels there?" His voice was dry.

"Probably not." She flipped the stopper and made a production of adjusting the water temperature. "You going to stand there and watch, or help?" Then she tucked her tongue between her teeth, reminding herself that Rome hadn't been built in a day. The Christmas tree? The noisy pizza joint with Layla banging the table and spilling his beer?

Miracles had already happened. It was greedy—foolish—of her to want more.

His boot slowly moved forward. "We should be doing this in my bathroom," he murmured when he crouched down beside her. "Lot more room there." His shoulder bumped hers. "Now what?"

Maddie quickly shut off the water, hoping he wouldn't notice her shaking hands. "Make sure the water isn't too hot for her."

"How am I supposed to know what's too hot for her?"

"Oh, for heaven's sake." She grabbed his hand and splashed it into the water. "Is it too hot for you?"

His gaze slid over her and she nearly stopped breathing. Beneath the warm water, his palm rested against hers. "Feeling pretty hot to me."

Her mouth opened. But no words came. She quickly pulled her hand away from his and lifted Layla into the tub. Even before her toes made contact with the water, she started kicking and squealing. By the time she was sitting in the few inches, she'd churned up her usual miniature tidal wave.

"Holy——" Linc sat back when a cascade of water splashed up the side of the tub, right into his face.

Maddie laughed. "I guess that ought to cool Uncle Linc off, right, Layla?" She grabbed the small, soft washcloth and dunked it in the tub, shooting Linc a look. "Now you see why we need all the towels."

"What if she turns onto her stomach," Linc whispered, leaning over the crib as he lowered the baby onto the mattress. "That's supposed to be bad, right? Sleeping on their stomach?"

"She won't turn over," Maddie assured him.

They'd survived the bath. Another bottle. Another diaper.

"How do you know?"

"Because she hasn't learned how to, yet." She picked up the baby monitor and took his arm, pulling him away from the crib.

"Well, when's she going to learn?" He followed her into the hall.

"Sooner than you'll be ready for."

"It's two freaking o'clock." He threw himself down on the bed beside her.

Maddie shook her head, not wanting to lift her cheek from the pillow. But she peeled her eyes open enough to see him sprawled beside her. Jeans. No shirt. Arm tossed across his eyes. "You have a bed of your own. One that's not dinky."

"Too far," he muttered. He was holding the baby monitor in his hand. "How long's she going to sleep this time?"

She closed her eyes again. "Not long enough," she whispered.

* * *

"S'not my turn, babe," Linc murmured. He rolled over, essentially pushing her out of her own bed. The monitor was on the floor. No need for it when they could both hear Layla crying, plain as 5:00 a.m.

Maddie dragged herself out of bed, nearly tripping over the boots on the floor. His? Hers? Who could tell?

Another diaper.

Another bottle.

"Your turn next time," she whispered, crawling back into bed.

He grunted. His arm hooked over her waist and he buried his nose in her neck.

She should have noticed more, but her eyes were already closing.

The sun was warm through the window.

Maddie sighed luxuriously. Stretched her legs.

It wasn't the sun that was warm.

She opened her eyes. Felt the heavy arm around her.

She leaned forward carefully, remembering that the monitor was on the floor.

His thigh pushed against hers. "She's asleep. Miraculously." The monitor dropped from his other hand onto the mattress near her nose. "Be still."

When everything inside her was skittering around like oil in a hot skillet? "It's Monday. Don't you have to go to work?"

"Boss's privilege." His arm tightened. "Told you to be still."

As if. She tried to remember when he'd come in to lie on her bed. "Linc—"

He exhaled and grabbed her hands, rolling over her.

"I warned you. Morning breath coming in." His head lowered over hers.

There was no morning breath.

Only a long, slow, lazy kiss that made her dissolve.

"I shouldn't do this," she whispered when his hands slid beneath her sweater.

He didn't stop. "But I should." He pulled the sweater over her head. His intense eyes slid over like a warm caress.

"I don't, uh, don't know if it's ethical—" It was an excuse. Anything to stem the churning need that rose inside her as surely as Layla's bathwater flooded the floor every single time. "I'm Layla's care—" His mouth cut off her words.

She couldn't help the sound that rose in her throat when his hands slid away from hers, but only to make her jeans slide away, too.

"If you wake up Layla," he murmured against her throat, "I'm going to have to get rough here."

She shuddered, running her greedy fingers over his hot chest. If he stopped, she was going to get positively crazy. "I'm quaking in my boots," she managed almost soundlessly.

"You're not wearing any." He proved it by kissing his way down her thigh to her knee.

Neither was he, she realized dimly.

And then his kiss started upward again.

And then she simply quaked.

Chapter Thirteen

"Get your coat."

Maddie paused and looked down at the sink full of suds where she was washing their lunch dishes. "Um... can we finish here?" She rinsed the plate and held it toward him.

His eyes glinted and he dropped a kiss on her shoulder, ignoring the plate that he'd claimed he would dry. "I do like the way we finish."

She flushed. Not even the fact that Layla was strapped to the front of her kept warm, slippery heat from filling her. "You said you'd dry," she reminded him.

He grabbed the plate and gave it a cursory rub with the dishtowel. "It's dry. And next time use the dishwasher. That's what it's for." He took the sponge out of her hand and pulled her out of the kitchen.

She couldn't help laughing. "Linc!"

He brushed her lips with his, then ducked his head and brushed a kiss over Layla's nose. "Now go and get your coat."

"Why?"

His teeth flashed. "You'll see." He bolted up the stairs, taking them two and three at a time.

Maddie looked at Layla. "Who is that pod person who's taken over Uncle Linc? Hmm?"

Layla kicked and chortled. She grabbed Maddie's hair and gave a merry yank.

"Yeah, I like him, too," Maddie admitted quietly.

She more than liked him. She was stick stupid head over her heels for the man.

"You getting your coat?" Linc yelled from upstairs.

"Yes," she yelled back. They were hanging in the foyer. She tucked Layla into hers first, then strapped her into the fabric carrier before pulling on her own coat. She couldn't fasten the buttons, but with their combined body heat, she wasn't concerned. Then she covered the baby's head with Vivian's cap and hoped that it would stay there for more than a few minutes.

Maddie heard him on the stairs and turned to look.

And she was afraid that her heart would just crack right then and there.

Because he was carrying an old-fashioned wooden sled.

When he reached her, he leaned it against the door long enough to pull on his own coat. "It was in the attic, too." He picked it up again and opened the door. "Be lucky if it even glides. Runners haven't been waxed in God knows how long. But I figure it's worth a try."

She swallowed past the knot in her throat and followed him out onto the wide porch, down the brick steps and out onto the lawn where he dropped the sled in the snow. There was a short length of rope tied to the pointed front end. Probably the same rope that had been there when they were children. And it had been old, even then.

He stuck his boot down on the wood slats, experimentally pushing the sled back and forth. "Better than I expected."

She hugged her arms around Layla. She was kicking even more excitedly, as if she knew something fun awaited. Or maybe she was just keeping tempo with the chugging of Maddie's racing heart.

"Come on." He took the rope and gestured to the sled. "The chariot awaits."

Everything inside her wanted to get on that sled. But she hesitated. "I don't know. Layla—"

"I can't fit a car seat on the thing," he said dryly. "I'm just going to pull you around the yard, not hook you up to the back of the truck."

She crunched through the snow, waddling a little to keep her balance.

"You look like you're about twenty months pregnant with her strapped to the front of you like she is."

"Lovely." She knew her cheeks were red and blamed it on the cold. She was on the pill. But just the word "pregnant" made her thoughts zip where they had no business zipping.

She awkwardly straddled the sleigh and managed to sit down on it without falling on her butt. She adjusted Layla a little and crossed her legs atop the sled. "I don't remember this thing being quite so narrow."

He laughed softly. "You're still pretty damn cute on it, though." He grabbed the rope and started walking. "Hold on."

"To what?" She gasped as the sled jerked forward. "Layla or the sled?"

"Both." He walked a little faster. The runners began moving a little more smoothly. "I don't remember this thing being quite so heavy."

She scooped up a handful of snow and pelted the back of his head.

He jerked as it hit and looked back at her. He brushed snow out of his hair, his hazel eyes crinkling at the corners. "Good thing you've got Layla protecting you."

"Yeah, I'm really worried."

His expression turned downright wicked. "Quaking in your boots?"

She opened her mouth, but had no retort. Probably because all of her senses were swirling around in memories from that morning when they'd made love.

Then Layla squealed, kicking her feet, and Linc laughed again. He grabbed fresh hold of the rope and started running, dragging the sled and her heart merrily along.

They made it twice up and down the long, sloping yard and almost all the way out to the iron gate and back before Linc finally called it quits.

He pulled the sleigh up to the front of the house and dropped right onto his back in the snow. "That," he puffed, "is work."

Maddie unfolded her legs, groaning at how stiff they felt. "Nobody said you had to pull us for *miles*." Holding one arm around Layla, she managed to slide off the sled until she was on her back in the snow, too. She automatically pulled Layla's hat more firmly down over her ears. The afternoon sky was turning pale overhead. Clouds were starting to form. "But thank you."

She reached out her gloved hand until it bumped Linc. "That was—" *perfect* "—a lot of fun."

He bumped her back. "Thank you."

Her vision blurred and she blinked hard, willing it to clear.

But then his hand moved away and he sat up.

Only then did she realize a car was heading up the long driveway. She didn't even think a thing about it as she sat up, too, and watched it approach. Cold was seeping through her jeans by the time it reached the wide circle in front of the house and parked.

Then she scrambled to her feet when she recognized her cousin climbing from the vehicle.

"What's Justin doing here?" Linc stood also.

She swallowed. Her mouth had gone dry. She wrapped one arm around Layla, and reached for him with her other. "He must have the DNA comparison." She couldn't imagine any other reason why he would have made the drive to Braden.

Linc exhaled an oath. His hand tightened around hers, almost crushing her fingers. "He's not smiling."

She felt an abrupt urge to turn. To take Layla and just keep running.

But she didn't. She watched Justin head up the first set of shallow brick steps. Then the second. Until finally he stopped in front of them.

And she knew. Just from the solemn expression in his eyes.

"They're not a match," she said huskily.

Justin looked at Linc. "I'm sorry." He was holding an envelope in his hand. "I figured you'd want to know as soon as possible, but I couldn't make myself tell you over the phone. The woman at your office said you hadn't come in." He extended the envelope. "I know it's not what you were expecting. This is a copy of the report I've transmitted to the court."

Linc slowly released Maddie's hand before taking it. "This is a mistake."

"We ran them twice," Justin said. "I checked them personally. Even if Jax were here to compare—" He broke off, shaking his head. "I could cite all the technical jargon I explain in the report, but there is no way Layla is your brother's child, Linc. Not unless you and Jax have different biological fathers." He waited a beat. As if he hoped to hear it was possible. But Linc didn't even flinch. "You should have a certain percentage of half-identical DNA," he continued. "And you don't. It's not even close. I'm sorry."

Linc slowly sank down on the porch step. He stared at the unopened envelope in his hand. The hollow expression in his eyes was more than Maddie could bear.

Justin lightly touched Maddie's elbow. Sympathy was clear in his face. Then he turned and headed back to his car.

She watched him go through a glaze of tears.

Linc still hadn't moved, even when Justin's car was no longer in sight.

She sat next to him, pressing her cheek against Layla's head. She'd fallen asleep. At least she had no clue of the blow.

Maddie slid her hand over Linc's shoulder. "Linc. What Justin said. About you and Jax having different fathers—"

He finally stirred. "We don't." His voice came from somewhere very deep. "Out of all our parents' sins, that isn't one of them."

She chewed the inside of her cheek, wishing that such questions never needed to be asked. But his parents' infidelities were common knowledge. "How do you know for certain?"

"Ernestine," he said heavily. "She didn't like us hearing rumors. She made sure we knew who we were. Her grandsons."

"I'm sorry," she whispered.

"You warned me. I didn't listen." His voice went even lower. Rawer. "You need to leave me alone now, Maddie."

Her tears spilled over. She wiped them away and leaned toward him, pressing her mouth to his temple before she stood.

Then she carried the baby inside the house. Up the stairs past the Christmas tree. Beyond the tilted star. Into the nursery.

She carefully unwound herself from her coat and the multistrapped carrier, finally unveiling the baby. She didn't put Layla in the crib, though. She just sat down in the upholstered chair and held her close.

Because now there really was no guarantee how much longer she'd be able to hold her at all.

And without Layla, there would also be no reason for Maddie to stay.

"Take it all." Linc stood in the doorway of the nursery.

They'd just come from court.

Judge Stokes had been sympathetic. But inflexible.

They knew even less about Layla than they thought. If her mother—or father, whoever he might be—didn't step forward within the next ninety days, Layla would be eligible for adoption.

And the list of families waiting for a baby just like her was about a mile and a half long.

Even if Maddie and Linc got their names on the list, there were dozens ahead of them. The fact that they'd been caring for Layla for the past week and a half counted for nothing.

"The Perezes are a good couple." Her composure was tenuous as she packed Layla's clothes into a box.

Ray had taken Layla from them at the courthouse. Maddie had feared that Linc was going to physically assault her boss when he'd done so. But she knew that Ray was truly no happier about the result than she was. He'd even told her she could come back from vacation. He'd assign her as Layla's caseworker.

It was small comfort when she wanted to be so much more.

"They h-have two children of their own. Shelley—Mrs. Perez—used to be a nurse. Now, she's a stay-at-home mom. Steven is a school counselor. I've worked with them for…for years—" Her voice broke and she cleared her throat. "They're good fosters. They'll take excellent care of her." But she knew from experience how much space the Perezes had in their four-bedroom house. "They don't have room for any of this, though." She slowly closed the flaps of the box. "Except clothes and diapers—" Her voice broke again.

Linc crossed the room and pulled her against him. "I could still be a foster parent. Get qualified. If you married me, we'd be almost as good as the Perezes."

She buried her face against his chest. She couldn't bear his offer of marriage. "They won't be keeping her, either. Not once she's available for adoption."

His arms tightened. "There's still an investigation about who she is." His voice was rough. "Who left her. No matter what your cousin said about the profile, Jax is involved somehow. Layla's mother wouldn't have left her here with that note. If they'd just agree to hack his damn phone, there are messages. Phone calls. Something that would have to help."

"Jax isn't under suspicion for any wrongdoing. There's no presumption he's her father. He wasn't even here when she was left. The phone is a dead issue." She was simply repeating what the prosecutor had said. Because he, too, had been at the hearing.

Just one big, very unhappy family.

"I need to get Layla's things over to her." She swiped her face and pushed away from him. Her throat ached. Her heart ached. She looked up at him. "Are you going to be okay?"

His jaw tightened. "Are you?"

She swiped her cheek again. She picked up the box. "This is my job."

"It's more than your job. It's been more than your job from the second you asked your brother to call the judge."

"And look what good it's done."

He'd opened his heart to a baby girl, only to lose her.

"I'll pick up my things later."

"Terry can take care of it."

She felt like the hole inside her couldn't yawn any wider.

Without Layla, what purpose did she have there?

Humiliation at seventeen was nothing compared to heartbreak at thirty.

"Fine," she whispered. She carried the box past him. "Goodbye, Linc."

"What's going on? Somebody die?"

Linc looked up from the bottle of whiskey sitting in front of him. He blinked past the sandpaper in his eyes when the chandelier came on, dousing the gloomy living room in painful light. "Jax?"

His brother dropped his duffel bag on the floor, giving the Christmas tree a surprised look as he walked past it. "What're you sitting in the dark for?" He strolled closer and picked up the near-empty bottle. "Thought you gave that stuff up after Gram died."

Linc shot off his chair, grabbing his brother by his jacket. "Where the *hell* have you been?"

"Christ, Linc! What's—"

Linc shoved him. Hard. It was either that, or punch the hell out of him.

Jax landed in the leather chair behind him with a *whoosh*. He swore loudly and started to pop back up.

Linc lifted a warning hand. "Do. Not. Move."

Jax warily spread his palms in surrender and sat back in the chair. "How much *have* you had to drink?"

"Not anywhere near enough." Not enough to get Maddie's face out of his head. It had been four days since she'd carried that box out of his home and turned the place back into just a house. "You should have told me about Layla."

Jax's eyes narrowed. Unlike Linc's, they were blue. Very blue against his tanned face. "Layla." He waited a beat. "Afraid you'll have to be a little more specific."

Linc yanked the copy of the note he'd made out of his pocket. The edges where he'd folded it were creased and creased again from the number of times he'd studied it. He tossed it at his brother's head. "Layla."

"Eat some prunes, brother." Jax unfolded the note, but the words on it clearly made no impression. "So I ask again, who is Layla?"

Linc's ears buzzed. Maybe he was just going to have

a stroke. He'd leave Swift Oil to his brother, who'd either run it into the ground or not.

He rubbed his eyes with his palms, then dropped his hands. "Where have you been?"

Jax looked away. "Turks and Caicos."

"With Dana?"

His brother hesitated.

"She's going to ruin you one day," Linc said, sighing.

"Like she ruined you?"

"She's not the one who ruined me," he countered. "You should have just told me you were going. Or at least taken your damn phone." He picked up the note. "Someone left this for you."

"Who?"

"If I knew," Linc said through his teeth, "I wouldn't have cared where you were. Or how long you'd be."

"Man, you have lost your nut." Jax looked over at the tree. "What's with the whole merry, merry thing, anyway?"

"You'd lose your nut, too, if someone left a baby on your doorstep with just a *note* attached!"

Jax gaped. "What are you talking about?"

"Layla," Linc said. "The infant who was dumped on our doorstep two weeks ago. With that note to *Jaxie* attached!"

His brother shot out of his chair, finally looking alarmed. "Well, she wasn't *mine.*"

"I know that. Now." Linc sat, exhausted. It was his turn to watch his brother pace around the room for a while. "The DNA they did on us proved that."

"So what happened to the kid?"

"That *kid* has a name. Layla."

"Fine. What happened to *Layla*?"

He rubbed at the pain in his chest. It was worse than the ulcer had ever been. "She's gone."

"Gone." His brother turned pale. "Dead?"

"No!"

"Jesus Christ, Linc." Jax sat down, too. "Stop freaking me out!"

"She's with a foster family. And since you're not her father, we don't know *who* she is."

"Or where she belongs, I'm guessing," Jax murmured slowly.

"I know where she belongs." Linc closed his eyes and leaned his head back. Maddie's face swam behind his lids. Maddie laughing. Maddie crying. Maddie watching him through her lashes while she pulled him into her—

"Look, Linc." Jax picked up the copy of the note. "It's taken me more than twelve hours to get home. And following you is more than I can deal with. Why don't you start from the beginning."

So Linc did.

When he was finished, Jax silently reached for the bottle of whiskey. He didn't bother with a glass, just took a shot straight from the bottle. "Damn."

"All we have is that note."

His brother spread it over his thigh. "'Jaxie, please take care of Layla for me.'" The toe of his hiking boot bounced. "Jaxie. Nobody calls me that. 'Cept—" He made a face.

Linc almost grabbed Jax by the throat again. *"Except?"*

"Hold on. It'll come to me. She had a stripper name." Jax tapped his fingers against his forehead. Then he stopped and looked at Linc. "Miranda," he said. "Daisy Miranda. Waitressed for me," he frowned again, "for a few months. Over a year ago. She wasn't pregnant. Never said it, anyway. And damn sure didn't look it. But she did call me Jaxie."

Linc stood and pulled his brother out of his chair. "Come on."

"Where?"

"Magic Jax. You keep records of your employees, don't you?"

"Since my business partner frowns on it if I don't—" Jax rolled his eyes when Linc glared. "Yes, I keep records."

"Then we're going to get every piece of information you've got about Daisy Miranda and give it to Maddie. She'll know what to do with it."

"And have Daisy arrested for abandoning her kid?"

"Maybe. But at least Layla can't get adopted by somebody else before they have a chance to even find her real mother."

"Yeah, but why Maddie?"

Linc glared.

His brother lifted his hands. "Dude. Relax. It's like that, is it?"

"Yeah." He grabbed his coat and yanked open the door. "It's like that."

"What d'you know." Jax followed him out into the evening. "She always was a sweetheart."

Linc stopped in his tracks. "If you so much as look at her, I'll—"

Jax lifted his hands. "Not ever. Not again."

Linc unlocked his jaw. Dana was one thing. Maddie another. And he didn't want to have to kill his own brother.

"Just gotta say," Jax grinned a little crookedly. "It is good to know you've still got a heart."

Chapter Fourteen

"I don't think I've seen a longer face in all of my life." Vivian, dressed in shimmering silver, held a glass of amber liquid out to Maddie.

Maddie had no more interest in alcohol than she did in being at her grandmother's fancy Christmas party. But she tucked her phone behind her and took the glass anyway. One sip and her throat was on fire. It might have felt a little less potent if she'd spent more time eating something of substance versus pointlessly staring at the photo she'd taken of Linc and Layla. "I didn't think anyone would notice I slipped out. I certainly don't want to take you away from your own party."

She was sitting in Vivian's sunroom. *Conservatory*, as her grandmother insisted on calling it. Whatever. It was a window-lined room filled with exotic plants that had no business whatsoever flourishing in the middle of a Wyoming winter. But thanks to her grandmother's

fancy lighting and the air she probably had bottled and
flown in from the tropics, they did. And the silent plants
were better companions than the guests who were filling the two-story atrium at the center of Vivian's enormous house.

If Maddie could have blocked out the sounds of the
Christmas music being played by a trio that her eccen-
tric grandmother had hired out of Phoenix, of all places,
she'd have been even happier in her misery.

"I notice lots of things," Vivian said. "And since it
is my party, I get to do as I please." She sipped at the
other glass she'd been carrying as she arranged herself
on one of the padded metal settees that dotted the conservatory. "Not that I need a party to do as I please,"
she added wryly.

Maddie smiled, as Vivian clearly meant her to do.
She took another sip of the burning whiskey.

It made her think of Linc.

Putting down the glass wouldn't matter, though.

Not when everything made her think of Linc.

"I had an interesting lunch the other day," Vivian
said. "With Horvald Stokes."

Maddie quickly set down the glass before she
dropped it. "What? Why?"

"I wanted to see if he had a price."

"Vivian!" Maddie shoved out of her chair, nearly
tripping over the long blue dress that she'd borrowed
from Hayley. She'd heard time and again from her dad
about his mother's manipulative nature, but had never
seen it in action. "You can't be serious."

"Calm down." Her grandmother picked up Maddie's
glass and handed it to her once more.

"I won't calm down." Agitated, she snatched the
glass and tossed back the contents, then had to lean

over as she coughed through the pain of it. "What…
possessed…you?" Her stomach churned.

Vivian leisurely sat back against the settee. "He
doesn't," she said. "Have a price, that is. I quite liked
that about him, actually."

"Judge Stokes is happily married, Vivian. Don't be
looking for a fifth husband there."

Her grandmother chuckled softly. "I have no desire
for a fifth. I'm quite content knowing I had the best
in Arthur. And very aware that he could have done so
much better than me." She sobered. "Sadly, I can't help
you or your Lincoln where the baby is concerned. But
I wanted to."

Maddie's eyes stung. "He's not my Lincoln. And
Layla—"

"Isn't anyone's." Vivian sighed. "Heartbreaking, really."

Maddie pinched the bridge of her nose. "I'm really
not up to doing this," she whispered.

"Your mother seems to think you're in love with
him."

The musical trio was singing "Have Yourself a
Merry Little Christmas." The same song that had been
playing when she and Layla had visited Linc at his office. Her chest ached even more. "It doesn't matter."

Vivian tsked. "Of course it matters."

"He doesn't love *me*, Vivian. He only proposed because—"

"Proposed!" Vivian sat forward, like a cat pouncing.

"Don't get excited. It was only because he thought it
would improve his chances of keeping Layla. I promise
you, I set him straight." She was nauseated just thinking about it. Or maybe it was the whiskey on an empty
stomach.

"Did you now."

"What's that supposed to mean?"

"I once thought I set Arthur straight. He brought me around to his thinking, of course. But I wish that I'd never wasted all that time that we could have spent together before he did. We had little enough of it together in the end."

"This is not the same situation, Vivian. I turned him down." Four times. Four times, she'd turned him down. "Linc's not the kind of man to get over that."

"Of course not, dear. No doubt, he is the most unforgiving soul there ever was." She held out her hand. "Help me up. I'm neglecting my other guests."

Maddie quickly took her arm and helped her rise, even though she had the strong sense that Vivian needed no assistance whatsoever. "He's not unforgiving," she muttered.

"Whatever you say, dear." Vivian patted her cheek. "When you're tired of drinking among the palms, come back out and join us."

Then she gathered her shimmering dress and swept out of the room.

Maddie exhaled. She had nothing left to drink among the palms. She followed her grandmother.

The tree in the center of the atrium was taller than the one she and Linc had cut. More slender and more perfectly manicured.

She stopped in front of it, looking up at all the crystal and gold. But in her mind, she was seeing one with faded nutcrackers and a lopsided star.

"You were right. It's an art piece."

Maddie jerked, whirling around. "Linc." He was looking very un-Linc-like. His eyes were bloodshot.

His hair fell over the lines in his forehead. His jeans looked ancient and his shirt was wrinkled.

And he still was the best sight in the room.

"Does Vivian know you're here?"

"Yeah. I saw her a few minutes ago. Didn't seem to mind me crashing too much."

Behind him, she saw her grandmother smiling as she crossed the room. "I'll bet she didn't." She crossed her arms over the front of her low-cut dress that she didn't fill out anywhere as well as Hayley and turned to face the tree again. "What are you doing here?"

"Jax is back."

Her jaw loosened. She dropped her arms and turned toward him. The lights around them danced dizzily. "What?"

"He knows who wrote the note."

It was as though his voice was suddenly coming through a tunnel. She blinked. "Layla's note." Of course he meant Layla's note. What other note was there?

His hands closed around her shoulders. "Are you all right? You look like you're—"

"—*fine*," she cut him off, shrugging away from his touch. She bumped the tree behind her, and crystal and gold shimmered and tinkled. "I am...*fu-hine*."

And to prove it, her eyes rolled and she pitched forward, straight into his arms.

"Well." Linc sat on the edge of the couch where he'd deposited her. "I guess we know who gets to be the fireworks at your grandmother's party this year." He handed her a glass. "Water."

Maddie peered at him. Her mouth felt like cotton. She took the water and drained it. She didn't recognize the room. Nor could she hear the Christmas trio anymore. Between knocking into the tree and realizing he was carrying her into this room, everything was blank. "Please tell me I didn't yack on Vivian's marble floor or something."

"It was a pretty straightforward passing out, actually." His fingers grazed her hand and he stood. "I'll be back in a minute." He walked over to the door and she could hear him talking to someone, though his voice was too low to tell what he said.

She pressed her arm over her eyes. "Top of your game, Maude," she murmured.

After a moment, he returned and sat back down on the edge of the couch, his hip crowding her thighs. "Nice dress."

She self-consciously tugged the bodice. "It's Hayley's. No time to alter it. Who was at the door?"

"Your mom. She knows you're okay."

Maddie could only imagine.

Mrs. Lincoln Swift.

She struggled awkwardly to sit. Considering her long skirt was caught under him, it was an effort in futility. She gave up and stared at him. "You said Jax is back. He knows who wrote the note."

"A cocktail waitress. Worked for him for a short time over a year ago. Daisy Miranda."

The name meant nothing to her. "Layla Miranda," she murmured. She suddenly pushed at him again. "Let me up. I need to get in touch with Ray. And Judge Stokes. And the Prosecutor's Office."

His hands pushed her back down. "All of that is being done. Ali. Greer. Archer. They're all doing their part."

She subsided. "This is good news, Linc, but—"

"I know. It doesn't mean anything changes where Layla and you and I are concerned."

Her eyes stung. "I wish I could have made everything work out. For everyone."

"You can't fix everything."

"If there's a chance of locating Daisy, Judge Stokes will hold off placing her for adoption as long as he can. Which means she'll need more long-term foster care than we planned. And it's not unheard of for people to end up adopting a child they've fostered. Stokes has never approved it, but I... I can at least help you get qualified as a foster parent. Prove to Judge Stokes that you are the best one for Layla even if you aren't married. I mean, it's an old-fashioned notion and it's high time he—"

He pressed his hand over her lips.

"—started realizing it," she mumbled, too far gone to stop.

"You can't fix everything," he repeated softly.

"I know, but—"

"But you can fix me."

She stared at him above his big, warm hand.

"I know I'm nowhere near good enough for you, Maddie Templeton. But I'll do my damnedest to try. Just say you'll marry me." He cautiously pulled his hand away.

Her heart charged inside her chest. "Layla—"

"This isn't about Layla. I want her in our life. And we'll figure out how to make that happen. But this is about *me*. And *you*. And the fact that my house hasn't been the same since the day you left it."

"You don't love me," she whispered. "You can't possibly."

His eyebrows lifted. "Because I don't have parents who're still besotted with each other to have shown me how?"

"*No!* You're so much better than that. You're good and you care so *much* about doing what's right—"

He covered her mouth again. But this time, with just his thumb. "—and I love you." His thumb glided along her lip, then made way for his kiss. "Just tell me there's a chance you could love me back," he whispered. "And I'll be happy to break Gus's record every day of the week until you say yes."

She stared up at him, her eyes searching. She wanted so desperately to believe. "I loved you when I was seventeen." She shakily touched his cheek, brushed his tumbled hair back from his eyes. "I never knew how much I could love you now."

"What are you saying?"

It was the hope that got her. It lit his hazel eyes. It heated her through to her soul. She didn't need to be at the top of her game with him.

She just needed to be. With him.

"I'm saying five times is enough, Lincoln Swift." She lifted her mouth to his. "I'm saying yes."

Maddie stole a glance over her shoulder before leaning her head closer to Linc. "Stop fidgeting," she whispered.

He stretched his arm along the crowded church pew behind her and leaned his head closer to hers. "This is the longest Christmas Eve service in the history of time."

She bit her lip, trying not to smile. It was true. The church service—dominated by the children's pageant—had been dragging on longer than usual. Which was good, because Ray had promised to get there before it ended.

She slid her fingers between Linc's. "Just imagine Layla singing in a children's choir like this one day."

He made a low sound and shifted again. "Swift Oil's gonna donate padded seats," he whispered.

She ducked her chin, muffling her quick laugh and stole another look toward the back of the church.

Still no Ray.

"Hey." Ali sat forward from her spot on the pew behind them, and stuck her head between theirs. "Quiet down. Mayor's giving you guys the stink eye."

Maddie's shoulders shook. "Shh."

Grinning wickedly, and satisfied with her results, Ali sat back. They were all there. Ali. Greer. Her parents. Even Hayley and Seth.

Linc's hand went from the pew to Maddie's shoulder. "She's right," he murmured against her cheek. "Big-time stink eye. I always knew it was more interesting sitting over here with your family."

She closed her eyes and prayed that they wouldn't be struck with lightning for not showing the proper reverence while three toddler-size Wise Men tripped over their robes as they made their way to the manger.

"Let's go to Vegas," he whispered. "We can be married by morning."

Her lips parted. For a moment, she forgot all about her boss as she looked at Linc. "Now?"

"Unless you want the whole hometown wedding thing."

A wedding there meant time wasted through the holiday, waiting for a marriage license. Time that could be spent together. As his wife. Right now. Or at least as soon as he could get them to Las Vegas.

Considering he had resources upon resources, she wasn't too concerned on that front.

"Mrs. Lincoln Swift," Maddie murmured. She pressed her lips to his. "All I want is you." There was no doubt. No hesitation at all. "But maybe we should at least wait until the service is over."

This time, Meredith leaned forward. "Shh." But her eyes were sparkling.

And Linc wasn't the least bit cowed. "Let's do it now." Holding her hand, he stood.

Following seemed simpler than arguing. At least right there in the middle of the kids breaking into another Christmas carol. She felt certain it was their twentieth. Murmuring apologies as she went, she slowly followed him out of the crowded pew, Linc's hand in one hand, her coat in the other. Once they were free of the bodies, though, she didn't even care that they'd become the focus of the congregation as they hurried out.

Because Judge Stokes and his wife were hurrying in. And he gave Maddie a benevolent smile as they slipped into the standing-room only space at the rear of the church.

She relaxed a little. If Stokes was there, she knew Ray would soon follow.

Snow was drifting from the sky when they slipped out the church doors. Linc helped her on with her coat and kept hold of the collar. "I love you, Maddie."

Her heart skittered. She reached up and brushed a snowflake from his hair. "I love you, too. But before we go to Vegas, there's something I need to tell you. Something that just came up today, actually."

He hooked his hands behind her back. "There's nothing you can tell me that's going to slow us down or keep us going to from Vegas. I want you *all* to myself."

Delight shivered through her. If she hadn't spotted

her boss just then, she might well have forgotten everything except Linc. "No sharing?"

"*No* sharing."

She reached up and brushed her lips against his. "You might want to rethink that." She pushed his shoulder until he turned enough to see Ray.

Heading toward them. Obviously carrying something.

Some*one*.

She felt Linc go still. His hand tightened on hers. "What's going on?"

"Shelley Perez's sister went into premature labor this afternoon." She bit her lip. "She needed to leave town to be with her. And, well—"

Ray stopped in front of them, looking typically out of breath. "Figured I'd get here before this, but it took a while for Steven to get Layla's clothes together." He grinned and handed over the baby. She was dressed in her tiny white coat, a familiar red cap covering her head.

Even though she'd been expecting the baby, tears still blurred Maddie's vision as she clasped Layla to her chest. The baby smacked her chin and chortled.

"I don't understand." Linc's voice was gruff. His hand shook as he covered Maddie's.

She met his gaze. "With Shelley Perez out of town indefinitely because of her sister, her husband can't handle their kids and an infant all on his own. Which means Layla needs new foster care."

"And now there's some information about her mother to actually investigate," Ray inserted. "Which is why, a few minutes ago, Stokes agreed to name you both joint custodians until we can get more answers."

"*Both* of us!" Maddie hadn't expected that. "He's never done anything like that before!"

Ray winked. "Even judges get a little Christmas spirit." He patted the baby's arm. "I'll get her stuff from my car." He walked away.

"I can't believe this," Linc said. "You *knew* this was happening?"

"Not about the joint custodianship, but yes." She smiled tremulously. "It's not permanent, but it's something."

"It's everything." Linc's arms surrounded them both. "And *you* are amazing."

She lifted Layla higher. "Say Merry Christmas to Uncle Linc, baby."

Layla kicked and chortled. She reached for Linc's face. He caught her tiny mittened hand and kissed it. Then he kissed Maddie. And the sweetness that slid through her veins was going to last a lifetime.

"This changes things about Vegas." His voice was husky. "We'll get a license when the holidays are over. Get married at the courthouse."

"We could do that," she allowed. "But you know, we *do* have a church and a judge right here who's evidently in the holiday spirit…"

Linc threw back his head and laughed. Then he grabbed Maddie's hand and tugged her back toward the church.

* * * * *

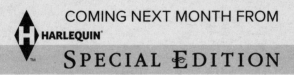
Available December 19, 2017

#2593 HER SOLDIER OF FORTUNE
The Fortunes of Texas: The Rulebreakers • by Michelle Major
When Nathan Fortune returned home, he vowed to put the past behind him. But when Bianca, his best friend's little sister, shows up with her son, Nate finds that the past won't stay buried...and it threatens to snuff out the future Nate and Bianca now hope to build with each other.

#2594 THE ARIZONA LAWMAN
Men of the West • by Stella Bagwell
Tessa Parker goes to Arizona to investigate her unexpected inheritance and gets more than a ranch. There's a sexy deputy next door and perhaps this orphan may finally find a family on the horizon.

#2595 JUST WHAT THE COWBOY NEEDED
The Bachelors of Blackwater Lake • by Teresa Southwick
Logan Hunt needs a nanny. What he gets is pretty kindergarten teacher Grace Flynn, whose desire for roots and a family flies right in the face of Logan's determination to remain a bachelor. Can Logan overcome his fears of becoming his father in time to convince Grace that she's exactly what he wants?

#2596 CLAIMING THE CAPTAIN'S BABY
American Heroes • by Rochelle Alers
Former army captain and current billionaire Giles Wainwright is shocked to learn he has a daughter and even more shocked at how attracted he is to her adoptive mother, Mya Lawson. But Mya doesn't trust Giles's motives when it comes to her heart and he will have to work harder than ever if he wants to claim Mya's love.

#2597 THE RANCHER AND THE CITY GIRL
Sweet Briar Sweethearts • by Kathy Douglass
Running for her life, Camille Parker heads to her sworn enemy, Jericho Jones, for protection. She may be safe from those who wish her harm, but as they both come to see their past presumptions proven incorrect, Camille's heart is more at risk than ever.

#2598 BAYSIDE'S MOST UNEXPECTED BRIDE
Saved by the Blog • by Kerri Carpenter
Riley Hudson is falling for her best friend and boss, Sawyer Wallace, the only person who knows she is the ubiquitous Bayside Blogger. Awkward as that could be, though, they both have bigger problems in the form of blackmail and threats to close down the newspaper they both work for! Will Sawyer see past that long enough to make Riley Bayside's most unexpected bride?

YOU CAN FIND MORE INFORMATION ON UPCOMING HARLEQUIN® TITLES, FREE EXCERPTS AND MORE AT WWW.HARLEQUIN.COM.

HSECNM1217

Get 2 Free Books,
Plus 2 Free Gifts—
just for trying the Reader Service!

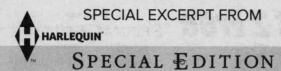
"He's an idiot," Nate offered automatically.

One side of her mouth kicked up. "You sound like Eddie. He never liked Brett, even when we were first dating. He said he wasn't good enough for me."

"Obviously that's true." Nate took a step closer but stopped himself before he reached for her. Bianca didn't belong to him, and he had no claim on her. But one morning with EJ and he already felt a connection to the boy. A connection he also wanted to explore with the beautiful woman in front of him. "Any man who would walk away from you needs to have his—" He paused, feeling the unfamiliar sensation of color rising to his face. His mother had certainly raised him better than to swear in front of a lady, yet the thought of Bianca being hurt by her ex made his blood boil. "He needs a swift kick in the pants."

"Agreed," she said with a bright smile. A smile that

made him weak in the knees. He wanted to give her a reason to smile like that every day. "I'm better off without him, but it still makes me sad for EJ. I do my best, but it's hard with only the two of us. There are so many things we've had to sacrifice." She wrapped her arms around her waist and turned to gaze out of the barn, as if she couldn't bear to make eye contact with Nate any longer. "Sometimes I wish I could give him more."

"You're enough," he said, reaching out a hand to brush away the lone tear that tracked down her cheek. "Don't doubt for one second that you're enough."

As he'd imagined, her skin felt like velvet under his callused fingertip. Her eyes drifted shut and she tipped up her face, as if she craved his touch as much as he wanted to give it to her.

He wanted more from this woman—this moment—than he'd dreamed possible. A loose strand of hair brushed the back of his hand, sending shivers across his skin.

She glanced at him from beneath her lashes, but there was no hesitation in her gaze. Her liquid brown eyes held only invitation, and his entire world narrowed to the thought of kissing Bianca.

"I finished with the hay, Mommy," EJ called from behind him.

Don't miss
HER SOLDIER OF FORTUNE by Michelle Major,
available January 2018 wherever
Harlequin® Special Edition books and ebooks are sold.

www.Harlequin.com

THE WORLD IS BETTER WITH

Romance

Harlequin has everything from contemporary, passionate and heartwarming to suspenseful and inspirational stories.

Whatever your mood,
we have a romance just for you!

Connect with us to find your next great read, special offers and more.

f /HarlequinBooks

🐦 @HarlequinBooks

www.HarlequinBlog.com

www.Harlequin.com/Newsletters

HARLEQUIN®

A *Romance* FOR EVERY MOOD™

www.Harlequin.com

Looking for more satisfying love stories
with community and family at their core?

Check out **Harlequin® Special Edition**
and **Harlequin® Western Romance** books!

New books available every month!

CONNECT WITH US AT:

Harlequin.com/Community

 Facebook.com/HarlequinBooks

Twitter.com/HarlequinBooks

Instagram.com/HarlequinBooks

Pinterest.com/HarlequinBooks

ReaderService.com

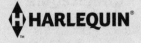

**ROMANCE WHEN
YOU NEED IT**

HFGENRE2017R